Large Print Ste
Steele, Jessica.
His pretend mistress

HIS PRETEND
MISTRESS

HIS PRETEND MISTRESS

BY

JESSICA STEELE

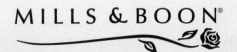

MILLS & BOON®

*First published in Great Britain 2002
Large Print edition 2002
Harlequin Mills & Boon Limited,
Eton House, 18-24 Paradise Road,
Richmond, Surrey TW9 1SR*

© Jessica Steele 2002

ISBN 0 263 17349 6

*Set in Times Roman 16½ on 17½ pt.
16-0802-52461*

*Printed and bound in Great Britain
by Antony Rowe Ltd, Chippenham, Wiltshire*

CHAPTER ONE

SHE was panicking so wildly she could barely manage to turn the knob of the stout front door.

Her employer—soon to be her ex-employer—coming into the hall after her gave her extra strength. 'Don't be so...' he slurred, but Mallon was not waiting to hear the rest of it. With shaking hands she yanked the door open and, heedless of the torrential rain deluging down, she went haring down the drive.

She did not stop running until her umpteenth glance behind confirmed that she was not being followed.

Some five minutes later Mallon had slowed to a fast walking pace when the sound of a motor engine alerted her to the fact that Roland Phillips might have decided to pursue her by car. When no car went past, panic started to rise in her again.

There was no one else about, nothing but acres and acres of unbuilt-on countryside so far as she knew. As the car drew level she cast a

5

jerky look to her left, but was only a modicum relieved to see that it was not Roland Phillips.

Had she been hoping that the driver would be a female of the species, however, she was to be disappointed. The window of the car slid down, and she found herself staring through the downpour into a pair of hostile grey eyes.

'Get in!' he clipped.

Like blazes she'd get in! She'd had it with good-looking men. 'No, thank you,' she snappily refused the unwanted offer.

The grey eyes studied her for about two seconds. 'Suit yourself!' the mid-thirties man said curtly, and the window slid up and the car purred on its way again.

Though not at any great speed, Mallon noticed as, shock from Roland Phillips's assault on her starting to recede a little, she also noticed that, with a veritable monsoon raging, only an idiot would drive fast in these conditions.

She trudged on with no idea of where she was making for, her only aim to put as much distance as possible between her and Roland Phillips at Almora Lodge. So far as she could recall there was not another house around for miles.

Her sandals had started to squelch, which didn't surprise her—the rain wasn't stopping; the sky was just emptying about her head.

That she was soaked to her skin was the least of her worries. She hardly cared about being drenched. Though she did begin to hope that another car might come by. If its driver was female Mallon hoped she would stop and give her a lift.

More of her shock receded and, feeling cold, wet, and decidedly miserable, Mallon half wished she had accepted a lift with the grey-eyed stranger.

A moment later and she was scoffing at any such nonsense. She'd had it with men; lechers, the lot of them! She had known some prime examples in her *ex*-stepfather, her *ex*-stepbrother, her *ex*-boyfriend, without the most recent example of that ilk, her *ex*-employer.

The rain pelted down, and, since she couldn't possibly become any more sodden, Mallon stopped walking and tried to assess her situation. She supposed she must have put a distance of about a mile or so between her and Almora Lodge. She had sprinted out of there dressed just as she was, in a cotton dress—too het up then to consider that this was probably the wettest summer on record—and without a thought in her head about nipping upstairs to collect her handbag. Her only thought then had been to put some space between her and the drunken Roland—call me Roly—Phillips.

Mallon resumed walking, her pace more of a dejected amble now as she accepted that, new to the area, she had no idea where she was going. Her only hope was that someone, foolhardy enough to motor out in such foul weather, would stop and offer her a lift.

Surely no one with so much as a single spark of decency would leave a dog out in such conditions, much less drive on by without offering her a lift?

Perhaps that was why the grey-eyed man had stopped? He hadn't sounded too thrilled at the notion of inviting her drenched person to mess up his leather upholstery. If, that was, his sharp-sounding 'Get in!' had been what you could call an invitation.

Well, he knew what he could... Her thoughts broke off as her ears picked up the purring sound of a car engine. She halted—the rain had slackened off a little—and she turned and watched as the car came into view.

She eyed the vehicle warily as it drew level, and then stopped. The window slid down—and at the same time the heavens opened again. Solemn, deeply blue eyes stared into cool grey eyes. He must have driven in a circle, she realised.

The man did not smile, nor did he invite her into his car, exactly. What he did say, was, 'Had enough?'

Mallon supposed that, with her blonde hair plastered darkly to her head, her dress clinging past saturation to her body and legs, she must look not dissimilar to the proverbial drowned rat.

She gave a shaky sigh. It looked as though she had two choices. Tell him to clear off, when heaven alone knew when another car would come along, or get into that car with him. He looked all right—but that didn't mean a thing.

'Are you offering?' she questioned jerkily.

His answer was to turn from her and to lean and open the passenger door. Then, as cool as you please, he pressed a button and the driver's window began to close.

Feeling more like creeping into some dark corner and having a jolly good howl, Mallon hesitated for only a moment or two longer. She still felt wary, but she also felt defeated.

She crossed in front of the vehicle and got in beside the stranger. When he stretched out his hand nearest her she jumped nervously. The man gave her a sharp glance, her wariness of him not missed, she gathered. Then he completed his intention of turning on the heater and directing the warmth on to her.

Instinctively she wanted to say she was sorry—but for what? She roused herself—all men were pigs; he would be no exception, and she would be a fool to think otherwise.

They had driven about half a mile when he asked, 'Where are you going?'

The car had a good heater and she supposed she could have thanked him for his thoughtfulness. But she didn't want to get into conversation with him. 'Nowhere,' she answered tiredly.

He gave a small snort of exasperation. 'Let me put it another way. Where would you like me to drop you?'

He was exasperated? Tough! 'Anywhere,' she replied. She hadn't a clue where she was going, where she was, even—none of the area was familiar territory.

He turned his head, grey eyes raking her. 'Where have you come from?' he questioned tersely.

She was feeling warmer than she had been, and while she was still wary, she felt a shade more relaxed. To her ears this man was sounding a touch fed up because he had bothered to act as any decent human being would to a fellow person and had bothered to pick her up at all. But she had a feeling that if she didn't soon answer he would open the door and tip her out. It was warm in the car. Somehow she felt too beaten to want to squelch out in the rain again.

'Almora Lodge,' she said. 'I've come from Almora Lodge.'

She wondered if he knew where Almora Lodge was, but realised he probably did when he asked, 'Do you want me to take you back there?'

'No, I don't!' she answered sharply, tartly. She drew a very shaky breath, and was a degree more in control when she added. 'No, thank you. I don't want to go back there— ever.'

Again she felt grey eyes on her, but v suddenly too tired and too emotionally hausted to care. He said nothing, howeve motored on for a couple of miles, and then started to slow the car down.

Alarm rocketed through her. Apart from a large derelict-looking building to the right, which stood in what looked like the middle of a field, there seemed to be no other dwelling for miles.

He slowed the car right down and steered it to what appeared to be the only respectable part of the derelict property—mainly the stone pillars either side of a gateless entrance that declared 'Harcourt House'.

'Where are you taking me?' she cried fearfully, her imagination working overtime. She could lie buried for years in the rubble hereabouts, or in one of those about-to-fall-down-looking outbuildings, and no one would be any the wiser!

In sharp contrast to her panicking tones, however, his tone was calm and even—if a shade irritated. 'Like Sinbad, I appear to be lumbered,' he answered, which—recalling the ale of the old man of the sea who refused to t off Sinbad's back—she didn't think was y complimentary. 'You don't know where want to go, and I'm not in the mood to play guessing games. I'm stopping off here to pick up some of my gear and...

'You live here!' she exclaimed in disbelief.

'I live in London. I'm having this place re-built,' he said heavily, going on, 'I hadn't intended to come down this weekend, but with this rain forecast I came down last night to check if a bad part of the roof had been made sound.' That, it appeared, was all the explanation he had any intention of making. Because he was soon going on, 'I've a couple of things to do inside that may take some while—you can either stay in the car incubating pneumonia until I can drop you off at the first shelter for homeless persons I come to, or you can come inside and dry off what's left of your frock while you wait for me in a heated kitchen.' So saying, he drove round to the rear of the house and braked.

Mallon stared at him for several stunned seconds, the homeless persons bit passing her by as her glance went from him and down over her dress.

With horrified eyes she saw that her dress was torn in several places. The worst tear was where the material had been ripped away in her struggle, and her bra, now transparent from her soaking, was clearly revealing the fullness of her left breast—the pink tip just as clearly on view.

'Oh!' she cried chokily, her cheeks flushing red, tears of humiliation not far away.

'Don't you dare cry on me!' he threatened bracingly, about the best tone he could have used in the circumstances, she realised. 'Come on, let's get you inside,' he said authoritatively and, taking charge, was out of the car and coming round to open the passenger door.

She did not immediately get out of the car. She'd had one tremendous fright—she was not going to trust again in a hurry. Thankfully the rain had, for the moment, abated. The stranger was tall and he bent down to look at her as stubbornly, a hand hiding her left breast, she stayed where she was, refusing to budge.

'You won't…?' she questioned, and discovered she had no need to complete the sentence.

Steady grey eyes stared back at her and every bit as though she had asked, did he fancy her enough to try and take advantage? his glance skimmed over the wreck she knew she must look, and 'Not in a million years,' he said succinctly. Which, while not being in the least flattering, was the most reassuring answer he could have given her.

He left her to trail after him when she was ready, opening up the rear door and entering what she could now see was a property that was in the process of undergoing major rebuilding.

Mallon stepped from the car and, careful where she walked, picked her way over builders' paraphernalia. The rear hall was dark and littered with various lengths of new timber. It was a dull afternoon. Up ahead of her an electric light had been switched on. From this she knew that, electricians having been at work, Harcourt House was no longer as derelict as it had once been and, if the front of the house was anything to go by, it appeared still to be.

Holding her dress to her, she followed the light and found the grey-eyed man in the act of switching on an electric kettle in what, to her amazement, was a superbly fitted-out kitchen.

'Your wife obviously has her priorities sorted out,' Mallon commented, hovering uncertainly in the doorway.

'My sister,' he replied, opening one of the many drawers and placing a couple of kitchen hand towels on a table near Mallon. 'I'm not married,' he added. 'According to Faye...' he paused as if expecting the name might be familiar to her—it wasn't—'...the heart of the home is the kitchen. With small input from me, I left her to arrange what she tells me is essential.'

As he spoke, so Mallon began to feel fractionally more at ease with the man, though whether this was his intention she had no idea. She found she had wandered a few more steps into the room, but her eyes were watchful on him while he made a pot of tea.

'There's an electric radiator over there,' he thought to mention. 'Why not go and stand by it? Though, on second thoughts, since you can't stand there nursing your wet frock to you the whole time, why don't I go and find you a shirt to change into while you drink your tea?'

Mallon didn't answer him but, discovering a certain decisiveness in him, she moved out of the way when he came near her on his way out. She was still in the same spot when he returned, carrying a shirt and some trousers, and even a pair of socks.

'There's a drying machine through there—that will eventually be a utility room,' he informed her, and added, 'There's a lock on the kitchen door. Why not change while I go and check on a few matters?'

Mallon was in no hurry to change. She felt this man was being as kind as he knew how to be, but she wasn't ready any longer to take anyone at face value. Eventually she went over to the kitchen door and locked it, presuming that, since the place was uninhabited apart from work hours Monday to Friday when the builders must traipse in and out of the place, it had been a good idea to be able to lock in the valuable kitchen equipment.

Quickly, then, Mallon made use of the towels. She was past caring what she looked like when, not long afterwards, her dress tumbling around in the dryer, she was warm and dry in the garments the man had brought her. She was five feet nine inches tall, but he was about six inches taller. She rolled up the shirt sleeves and to prevent the trousers dragging on the floor she rolled the legs of those up too—but she was stumped for a while as to how to keep them up. That matter was soon resolved when, her brain starting to function again, she vaguely recalled that some of the timber in the hall had been kept together by a band of coarse twine.

By the time she heard the stranger coming back, she had the largest of the hand towels wound around her now only damp hair, and was feeling a great deal better than she had.

She found a couple of cups and saucers, discovering in the process of opening various cupboards until she came to the right one that his sister, Faye, had not only organised the kitchen but had stocked it with plenty of tinned and packet foods as well.

Mallon had unlocked the kitchen door, and as the man came in she informed him, half apologetically for taking the liberty, 'I thought I'd pour some tea before it became stewed.'

'How are you feeling now?' he asked by way of an answer, taking up the two cups and saucers and carrying them over to the large table. He pulled out a chair for her, but went round to a chair at the other side of the table and waited for her to take a seat.

'Warmer, dryer,' she replied, trusting him enough to take the chair he had pulled out for her.

'Care to tell me your name?' he asked when they were both seated. She didn't particularly—and owned up to herself that she had been so thoroughly shaken by the afternoon's happenings she didn't feel at her sunniest. 'I'm Harris Quillian,' he said, as if by introducing himself it might prompt her to tell him with whom he was sharing a pot of tea.

'Mallon Braithwaite,' she felt obliged to answer, but had nothing she wanted to add as the silence in the room stretched.

He drained his cup and set it down. 'Anything else you'd like to tell me?' he enquired mildly.

Not a thing! Mallon stared at him, her deep blue eyes as bright as ever and some of her colour restored to her lovely complexion. She drew a shaky breath as she began to realise that she owed this man more than a terse No. He need not have stopped and picked her up. He need not have given her some dry clothes to change into. She acknowledged that it was only because of the kindness of Harris Quillian that she now felt warm and dry and, she had to admit, on her way to having a little of her faith in human nature restored.

'Wh-what do you want to know?' she asked.

He shrugged, as though he wasn't all that much interested anyway, but summed up, 'You're a young woman obviously in some distress. Apparently uncaring where you go, apart from a distinct aversion to return to your last port of call. It would appear, too, that you have nowhere that you can go.' He broke off to suggest, 'Perhaps you'd like to start by telling me what happened at Almora Lodge to frighten you so badly.'

She had no intention of telling him anything of the sort. 'Are you a detective?' she questioned shortly.

He shook his head. 'I work in the city. I'm in finance.'

From the look of him she guessed he was high up in the world of finance. Must be. To have this place rebuilt would cost a fortune. She still wasn't going to answer his question, though.

He rephrased it. 'What reason did you have for visiting Almora Lodge in the first place?' Stubbornly she refused to answer. Then discovered that he was equally stubborn. He seemed set on getting some kind of an answer from her anyhow, as he persisted, 'Almora Lodge is almost as out of the way as this place.

You wouldn't have been able to get there without some form of transport.'

'You *should* have been a detective!' She was starting to feel peeved enough not to find Mr Harris-financier-Quillian remotely kind at all!

'What panicked you so, Mallon, that you shot out of there without time to pick up your car keys?'

'I didn't have time to pick up my car keys because I don't have a car!' she flared.

He smiled—he could afford to—he had got her talking. 'So how did you get there?'

She was beginning to hate this man. 'Roland Phillips picked me up from the station—three and a half weeks ago!' she snapped.

'Three...' Harris Quillian broke off, his expression darkening. 'You lived there?' he challenged. 'You lived with Phillips at Almora Lodge? You're his mistress!' he rapped.

'*No, I am not!*' Mallon almost shouted. 'Nor was I *ever*!' Enraged by the hostile suggestion, she was on her feet glaring at the odious Harris Quillian. 'It was precisely because I wouldn't go to bed with him that I had a fight with him today!' A dry sob shook her and at the instant Harris Quillian was on his feet. He looked about to come a step closer, perhaps to offer some sort of comfort. But Mallon didn't want any sort of comfort from any man, and she took a hasty step back. He halted.

The next time he spoke his tone had changed to be calm, to be soothing. 'You fought with him?' he asked.

'Well, in truth, I don't think he actually hit me.' Her tone had quieted too. 'Though I shouldn't be surprised if I'm not nursing a few bruises in a day or two from the rough way he grabbed me,' she admitted. 'It was more me fighting him off, fighting to get free of him. He'd been drinking but he'd lost none of his physical strength.'

'You managed to get free before…?'

'Y-yes.' Her voice was reduced to a whisper—she felt quite ill from just remembering. Then realised she must have lost some of her colour when her interrogator said, 'It might be an idea if you sat down again, Mallon. I promise I won't harm you.'

Whether he would or whether he wouldn't, to sit down again suddenly seemed a good idea. Some of her strength returned then, sufficient anyway for her to declare firmly, 'I don't want to talk about it.'

Harris Quillian resumed his seat at the other side of the table, then evenly stated, 'You've had a shock. Quite an appalling shock. It will be better if you talk it out.'

What did he know? 'It's none of your business!' she retorted.

'I'm making it my business!' he answered toughly. Just because he'd picked her up in a monsoon and given her shelter! He could go and take a running jump! 'Either you tell me, Mallon,' he went on firmly, 'or...' Mallon looked across at him, she didn't care very much for that 'or'. 'Or I shall have to give serious consideration...' he continued when he could see he had her full attention '...to driving you to the police station where you will report Roland Phillips's assault...'

'I'll do nothing of the sort!' Mallon erupted, cutting him off. While it would serve Roland Phillips right if the police charged him with assault, there were other considerations to be thought of. A charge of assault, and its attendant publicity, was something Mallon knew, even if she was brave enough to do it for herself, would cause her mother grave disquiet. But her mother, after many years of deep unhappiness, was only now starting to be happy again. Mallon wasn't having a blight put on that happiness.

Obstinately she glared at Harris Quillian. Equally set, he looked back. 'The choice,' he remarked, 'is yours.'

Mallon continued to glare at him. He was unmoved. What was it with him? she fumed. So he'd given her a lift, given her dry clothes to put on—she took her eyes from him. Her dress—albeit torn—would be dry by now. Her glance went to the kitchen windows, despair entering her heart—the rain was pelting down again with a vengeance!

'I worked for him,' she said woodenly.

'Roland Phillips?'

'He advertised for a live-in housekeeper, clerical background an advantage,' she answered. 'I needed somewhere to live—a live-in job seemed a good idea. So I wrote to apply.'

'And he wrote back?'

'He phoned. He works as a European co-ordinator for a food chain. He said he was seldom home, but...'

'You agreed to go and live with him, without first checking him out?' Harris Quillian questioned harshly.

'Hindsight's a brilliant tool!' she exploded sniffily, and started to feel better again—it was almost as if this determined man was recharging her flattened batteries. 'He said he needed someone to start pretty much straight away. Which suited me very well. He said he was married and...'

'You met his wife?' Quillian clipped.

'She was abroad. She works for a children's charity and had just left to visit some of their overseas branches. I didn't know that until I'd arrived at Almora Lodge, but it didn't bother me particularly. Roland Phillips works away a lot too. In fact I'd barely seen anything of him until this weekend.'

'Is this the first full weekend he's been home?'

Mallon nodded. 'He arrived late on Friday. He...'

'He?' Quillian prompted when her voice tailed off.

'He—well, he was all right on Friday, and yesterday too,' she added. 'Though I did start to feel a bit uncomfortable—not so much by what he said, but the innuendo behind it.'

'Not uncomfortable enough for you to leave, then, apparently!' Quillian inserted, and Mallon started to actively dislike him.

'Where would I go?' she retorted. 'My mother remarried recently—it wouldn't be fair to move in with them. Besides which I hadn't worked for Roland Phillips a full month yet. Without a salary cheque I can't afford to go anywhere.'

'You're broke?' Quillian demanded shortly, and Mallon decided that she *definitely* didn't like him. It was embarrassing enough to have to admit to what had happened to her, without the added embarrassment of admitting that, since she couldn't afford alternative accommodation, she had nowhere to rest her head that night. 'He forgot to leave any housekeeping. I used what money I had getting in supplies from the village shop a mile away.'

'You never thought to ask him for some housekeeping expenses?'

'What is this?' she objected, not liking his interrogation one little bit. But when he merely looked coldly back at her, she found she was confessing, 'It seemed a bit petty. I thought I'd leave it until he paid me my salary cheque and mention it then. Anyhow,' she went on abruptly, 'Roland Phillips had too much to drink at lunchtime and—and...' she mentally steadied herself '...and seemed to think I was only playing hard to get when I told him to keep his loathsome hands to himself. It was all I could do to fight him off. It didn't occur to me when I managed to get free to hang around to chat about money he owed me! I was through the door as fast as I could go.' Mallon reckoned she had 'talked out' all she was going to talk out. 'There!' she challenged hostilely. 'Satisfied?'

Whether he was she never got to know, for suddenly there was such a tremendous crash from above that they both had something else momentarily to think about.

A split second later and Harris Quillian was out in the hall and going up the stairs two and a time. Mallon followed. There was water everywhere. He had one of the bedroom doors open and Mallon, not stopping to think, went to help. Clearly the roof was still in bad shape somewhere, and with all that rain—that crash they had heard was a bedroom ceiling coming down.

'Where do you keep your buckets?' she asked.

An hour later, the mopping up completed, the debris in the bedroom confined to one half of the floor space, Mallon returned to the kitchen. In the absence of abundant floor cloths, she had used the towel from around her head to help mop up the floor.

Fortunately her hair was now dry, and she was in the act of combing her fingers through her blonde tresses when Harris Quillian came to join her. Whether it was the act of actually doing something physical, she didn't know, but she was unexpectedly feeling very much more recovered. Sufficiently, anyhow, to real- ise she had better assess her options more log- ically than she had.

'Thank you for your help,' Harris Quillian remarked pleasantly, his grey eyes taking in the true colour of her hair. 'You worked like a Trojan.'

Mallon couldn't say he had been a slouch either, tackling all the heavy lifting, fetching and carrying. 'It was a combined effort,' she answered. For all she knew she looked a sketch—tangled hair, any small amount of make-up she had been wearing long since washed away, not to mention she was wearing Quillian's overlarge shirt and trousers, and, thanks to paddling about in water upstairs, was now sockless. 'I'd better start thinking of what I'm going to do,' she commented as lightly as she could.

'So long as you don't think about going back to Almora Lodge!' Quillian rapped, at once all hostility.

Oh, did he have the knack of instantly making her angry! 'Do I look that stupid?' she flared. But, knowing she was going to have to ask his assistance, had to sink her pride and come down from her high horse. 'I was—er—wondering—um—what the chances were of you giving me a lift to Warwickshire?' she said reluctantly.

'To your mother's home?' he guessed.

'There isn't anywhere else,' she stated despondently.

'But you don't want to go there?'

'She's had a tough time. She's happy now, for the first time in years. I don't want to give her the smallest cause for anxiety. Especially in this honeymoon period,' Mallon owned. 'But I can't at the moment see what else I can do.'

There was a brief pause, then, 'I can,' he replied.

Mallon looked at him in surprise—wary surprise. 'You can?'

'Smooth your hackles for a minute,' he instructed levelly, 'and hear my proposition.'

'Proposition!' she repeated, her eyes darting to the door, ready to run at the first intimation of anything untoward.

'Relax, Mallon. What I have to suggest is perfectly above board.' She was still there, albeit she was watching his every move, and he went quickly on. 'You need a job, preferably a live-in job, and I, I've just discovered, appear to need—a caretaker.'

'A caretaker!' She stared at him wide-eyed. 'You're offering me a caretaker's job?'

'It's entirely up to you whether you want to take it or not, but, as you know, I'm having the place rebuilt. I could do with someone here to liaise with plumbers, carpenters, electricians—you know the sort of thing. Generally keep an eye on everything.' He broke off to insert, 'Someone to mop up when the roof leaks. I've just witnessed the way you're ready to pitch in when there's an emergency. Later on, I'll need someone here to oversee painters and decorators, carpet fitters, furniture arrivals.'

He had no need to go on; she had the picture. But she had just had one very big fright with one employer and, while it would suit her very well to caretake for a short time—it would give her the chance to have a roof of sorts over her head while she looked for another job—she had been gullible before.

'Where's the catch?' she questioned, trying not to think in terms of this being a wonderful answer to her problems. If she accepted this caretaking job it would mean that she wouldn't have to go and intrude on her mother and John Frost at this start of their married life together. She...

'Apart from the fact that this kitchen is about the most comfortable room in the house, there is no catch,' Harris Quillian replied. 'You and I have a mutual need...'

'Where would I sleep?' Mallon interrupted him suspiciously.

Grey eyes studied her for a second or two. 'You don't trust men, do you?' he said quietly.

'Let's say I've had my fill of men who seem to think that I just can't wait to get into bed with them!'

'You've had bad experiences apart from Phillips?'

Mallon ignored the question. Her experience with Roland Phillips was the worst, but she had no intention of telling Quillian of her ex-stepfather, ex-stepbrother nor her fickle-hearted ex-boyfriend.

'Where would I sleep?' she repeated stubbornly, vaguely aware that she must be seriously considering the job offer.

'At the moment there are only two bedrooms habitable—and they're not yet decorated. One should be sufficient for you,' Quillian stated. 'Though at present only one of the bedrooms has much furniture. Obviously it's my bedroom for when I stay weekends.' Again she darted a quick look to the door. 'But I'll be returning to London this evening, so it would be all yours until I can get another bed sent down—probably tomorrow or Tuesday.' She relaxed slightly, and he asked, 'You wouldn't mind being here on your own?'

'I'd welcome it!' she answered bluntly, truthfully, hardly able to believe this sudden turn of events.

'Good,' he said, and she warmed to him a little that he appeared not in the slightest offended that she had just as good as said that she wouldn't mind if he left her on her own right now—that she'd rather have his space too, than his company. 'Should you accept, I'll get my PA to arrange some furniture first thing in the morning. By the end of the week you would be comfortably set up in your own bedroom.'

'You'll be—here again next weekend?' she questioned stiltedly, and found herself on the receiving end of his steady grey-eyed look.

'Are you always this cagey?'

'Apparently not—or I wouldn't be in the situation I'm in now!'

He took that on board, then documented, 'So you're worried about me staying overnight in the same house with you?' Mallon made no answer, and after a moment he informed her, 'The reason I bought this place was so that, eventually, I'd have somewhere away from London to unwind at the weekends. Harcourt House is obviously far from finished, but if you'd agree to stay on, ready to contact me or my PA with any problems—more ceilings coming down, builders needing chasing, that sort of thing—then, should I come down on a Friday evening, or on a Saturday, I'd undertake to drive you to a hotel and come and collect you shortly before I go back to London again. How does that sound?'

'How long would it be for?' she enquired, realising she should be snatching at his offer, but traces of shock from the terrible fright she'd had were still lingering. 'When I get my head back together I shall want to look around for something more permanent,' she explained.

'I can't see the builders being finished in under three months. Though I wouldn't hold you to that length of time if you find the right job sooner.'

Mallon took a deep breath. 'I'd like to accept,' she said, before she could change her mind. And, the die cast, she suddenly again became aware of the way she was dressed. 'My clothes!' she exclaimed. 'I can't go around wearing your shirt and trousers for the next three months!'

'Then I suggest I drive you to Almora Lodge to collect your belongings,' Harris Quillian said coolly.

'You'd come with me to...?' she began fearfully.

His jaw jutted. 'I wouldn't contemplate letting you go on your own,' he grated positively, and took his eyes from her to glance at his watch. When he looked at her again, Mallon could not help noticing that there was a steel-hard glint in his eyes all at once. Then, to her absolute amazement, he icily announced, 'Apart from anything else, I think it's more than high time I went and had a word with my brother-in-law.'

Mallon stared at him speechlessly, her brain refusing to take in what it was he was saying. 'Brother-in-law?'

Harris Quillian moved to the kitchen door, all too obviously keen to be on their way. 'Roland Phillips,' he stated quite clearly, 'happens to be married to my sister Faye.'

Mallon looked at him open-mouthed. She could not remember just then all that she had said to Harris Quillian. But what she did know was that she had told him, exceedingly plainly, that his sister's husband had assaulted her with violating, adulterous intent!

Anger started to surge up in her—anger against Quillian. How dared he allow her to tell him all she had? He must have known that she would never have said a word to him about Roland Phillips had she know he was Roland Phillips's brother-in-law!

More, she realised, Harris Quillian had deliberately kept that information to himself to get her talking. Must have! He'd purposely... He... How *dared* he?

CHAPTER TWO

MALLON felt angry enough to bite nails in half. 'You should have said!' she erupted furiously. 'You let me tell you everything I did, while all the time…'

'It wasn't the truth?' he cut in sharply, entirely unmoved by her anger. 'You're saying now that you were lying?'

'I wasn't lying. You know full well I wasn't lying!' she retorted—did he think she went out walking in a cloudburst wearing only a cotton dress just for the fun of it?

'Then what the blazes are you getting so stewed up about?' Quillian demanded.

'Because, because…' She faltered. Then she rallied. 'I wouldn't have told you anything of what I had if I'd known you were related to him!'

'Only by marriage!' he gritted, the idea of being related by blood to that worm plainly offensive to him.

'You won't say anything to your sister?'

'Give me one good reason why I shouldn't.'

Mallon stared at him angrily. 'If you can't see that to tell her might do irreparable harm to her marriage...'

'Harm has already been done. My sister and that apology for a man separated three months ago.'

Mallon's anger went as swiftly as it had arrived. 'Oh,' she murmured. 'H-he never said. He let me think she, his wife, had only recently left on an overseas trip to do with her work.'

'Did you see any evidence of Faye being around?'

'We're back to hindsight again,' Mallon muttered wearily. '*Now*, now that I *know*, I can see that there hadn't been a female hand about the Lodge for some while.'

'It was in need of a clean and tidy-up when you arrived?'

Understatement. 'Let's say it was fairly obvious he hadn't advertised for a housekeeper a minute too soon. Are he and your sister legally separated?'

Harris Quillian shook his head. 'It's a trial separation as far as Faye is concerned. She's hoping that, once they're through what she terms a cooling-off period, they'll get back together again.'

'Oh, grief!' It amazed Mallon that anyone with a grain of intelligence should fall for, let alone want to marry and stay married to, a man like Roland Phillips. 'It won't help if you tell her about me,' Mallon said.

'You're suggesting that I don't tell her? You think it would be better for her to go back to him without being aware of what he's capable of?' Harris questioned grimly.

'She may well know, but love him enough to forgive…'

'What he tried to do to you is unforgivable!' Harris chopped her off harshly.

Mallon let go a shaky breath. 'I— w-wouldn't argue that,' she had to agree.

The subject seemed closed. 'Ready?' he said. 'We'll go and get your clothes.'

Mallon suddenly had an aversion to putting on the dress that Roland Phillips had tried to tear from her. She knew then that she would never wear it again. She wouldn't have minded borrowing a comb, but Harris wasn't offering, and she wouldn't ask. 'I look a sight,' she mumbled.

'Do you care?'

It annoyed her that he too thought she looked a sight! He needn't have agreed with her. 'Not a scrap!' she answered shortly, and, delaying only to put on her sodden sandals, she joined him at the door.

The nearer they got to Almora Lodge, though, and nerves started to get the better of her. So that by the time Harris had pulled up outside the house, she had started to shake.

'You'll come in with me?' she questioned jerkily when all those terrible happenings began to replay in her head, refusing to leave. Suddenly she felt too afraid to get out of the car.

'I'll be with you most every step of the way,' he replied, his expression grim.

The front door was unlocked. Harris didn't bother to knock but, tall and angry beside her, he went straight in. There was no sign of Roland Phillips.

'I'll be one minute,' Harris said. 'If you see Phillips before I do, yell.'

Mallon waited nervously at the bottom of the stairs while Harris headed in the direction of the drawing room. She waited anxiously when he went from her sight. Then she thought she heard a small short sound that might have been a bit of a groan, then a thud—but she had no intention of venturing anywhere to find out what it was all about.

And, true to his word, barely a minute later Harris appeared. He *was* with her every step of the way too as they went up the stairs. He stayed close by while she packed her cases and retrieved her handbag.

She had been all knotted up inside, certain that at some stage Roland Phillips would appear, if only to find out who was invading his property. But she was back in the car sitting beside Harris Quillian—and had seen nothing of her ex-employer. She started to feel better.

'Thank you,' she said simply as they left Almora Lodge behind.

'My pleasure,' he replied, and at some odd inflection in his tone, almost as if it *had* been a pleasure, Mallon found her eyes straying to his hands on the steering wheel. The knuckles on his right hand were very slightly reddened, she observed.

'You saw Roland Phillips, didn't you?' she exclaimed as the explanation for that groan and thud suddenly jumped into her head. 'It wasn't very nice of him to mark your hand with his chin like that!' The words broke from her before she could stop them.

'Worth every crunch,' Harris confirmed.

Mallon turned sideways in her seat to look at him. Firm jaw, firm mouth, steady eyes; she was starting to quite like him. 'You didn't need much of an excuse to hit him,' she commented, guessing that because, at heart, his sister wanted to get back with her husband, Harris had previously held back on the urge to set about Roland for the grief he had caused Faye. However, Roland's behaviour today had given him the excuse he had been looking for.

'True,' Harris answered. 'Unfortunately he was still half sozzled with drink, so I only had to hit him once.' She had to smile; it felt good to smile. By the sound of it, Roland Phillips had gone down like a sack of coals.

Harris carried her cases up the stairs when they arrived at Harcourt House. The two habitable bedrooms were side by side. He placed her cases in the room as yet without a bed, and showed her the other room.

'Faye has seen to it that there's plenty of bed linen, towels, that sort of thing, so I'll leave that side of it to you.' And, when Mallon stood hesitantly in the doorway, he went on casually, 'I'll arrange for locks to be put on both these bedroom doors tomorrow.' Then, taking up what was obviously his overnight bag, he announced, 'Now I should think about leaving.'

Mallon began to suspect he had a heavy date that night. She wished him joy. She went downstairs with him, looking forward to the moment when he would be gone and she could change out of his clothes and into her own.

'You've been very kind,' she began as he accompanied her into the kitchen. 'I don't quite honestly know what I would have done if you hadn't done a circle round and picked me up.'

'You're helping me too, remember,' he said, and, taking out his wallet, he handed her a wad of notes. 'In view of your past experience, I think it might be as well if you accepted your salary in advance rather than in arrears.'

'I don't want...' she began to protest.

'Don't give me a hard time, Mallon. I've an idea you're going to earn every penny—if only by keeping an army of builders supplied with tea and coffee.' He smiled then, about the second time Mallon had seen him smile. This time it had the strangest effect of killing off all thought of protest. 'While we're on the subject of sustenance, fix yourself dinner from anything you fancy in the cupboards. It's there for your use, so eat heartily.' His glance slid over her slender figure, her curves obvious even in her baggy outfit. Mallon stilled, striving to hold down a feeling of panic. Then her large, deeply blue and troubled eyes met his steady grey ones, and he was no longer smiling. 'You have a beautiful face, Mallon, and a superb figure.' He brought out into the open that which she was panicking about. 'And you've had one hell of a fright today. But, trust me, not every man you meet will be champing at the bit for your body.'

She swallowed hard. This man, while sometimes being curt with her, sharp with her, had also been exceedingly kind. 'As in—n-not in a million years?'

He laughed then, and suddenly she relaxed and even smiled at him. She knew he had recalled without effort that he had answered 'Not in a million years' when she had earlier delayed leaving his car in fear that he too might have wicked intent. 'Something like that,' he answered.

'Then go,' she bade him, but, remembering he was now virtually her employer, 'Sir,' she added.

And he, looking pleased that her spirit seemed to have returned, was unoffended. Handing her his business card, 'Contact me if you need to,' he instructed. 'You'll be all right on your own?' he questioned seriously. 'No fears?'

'I'll be fine,' she answered. 'Actually, I'm suddenly starting to feel better than I have in a long while.'

Harris Quillian stared down at her, studying her. Then, nodding approvingly, he took up his overnight bag and his car keys. 'I may be down on Friday,' he said, and was gone.

Her sleep was troubled by dark dreams that night. Mallon awoke a number of times, feeling threatened and insecure, and was awake again at four o'clock, although this time dawn was starting to break. And, with the light, she began to feel a little more secure.

She lay wide awake looking round the high-ceilinged uncurtained room. As well as not having curtains, the room was as yet uncarpeted, but there was a large rug on the floor and, against one wall, a large oak wardrobe.

Mallon could tell that, once the building work was completed, furniture and furnishings installed, Harcourt House would revert to what had once been its former glory. She liked big old houses—she had been brought up in one.

Her eyes clouded over. She didn't want to dwell on times past, but could not help but think back to her happy childhood, her loving and loved parents and the plans they had made for her future—all of which had turned to dust nine years ago.

She had been thirteen when she and her mother were wondering whether to start dinner without waiting for Mallon's father. He'd been a consultant surgeon and worked all hours, so meals had often been delayed. 'We'll start,' her mother had just decreed, when there had been a ring at the doorbell. Their caller had been one of his colleagues, come to tell them that Cyrus Braithwaite had been in a car accident.

The hospital had done everything they could to try and save him, but they must have known at the start from the extent of his injuries that they were going to lose him.

Mallon had been totally shattered by her adored father's death; her mother had been absolutely devastated and completely unable to cope. With the help of medication, her mother had got through day by day, but Mallon could not help but know that Evelyn Braithwaite would have been happier to have died with her husband—that perhaps it was only for her daughter's sake that she'd struggled on.

Some days had been so bad for her mother that Mallon would not consider going to school and leaving her on her own. The first year after her father's death had passed with Mallon taking more and more time off school. Her studies had suffered and, having been at the top of her year, her grades had fallen; but she'd had higher priorities.

Her father had been dead two years when her mother had met Ambrose Jenkins. He was the antithesis of Mallon's father: loud where her father had been quiet, boastful where her father had been modest, work-shy where her father had been industrious. But, at first, he'd seemed able to cheer her mother, and for that Mallon forgave Ambrose Jenkins a lot. She'd found she could not like him, but had tried her hardest to be fair, recognising that because she had thought so much of her father she could not expect any other man to measure up.

So when, within weeks of meeting him, her mother told her that she and Ambrose were going to be married, Mallon had kissed and hugged her mother and pretended to be pleased. Ambrose had had a twenty-seven-year-old son, Lee. Mallon had found him obnoxiously repellent. But, for her mother's sake, she'd smiled through the wedding and accepted that Ambrose would be moving into their home.

What Mallon had not expected was that Lee Jenkins would move in too. By then she was a blossoming fifteen-year-old, but, instead of being proud of her beautiful blonde hair and curvy burgeoning figure, Mallon had been more prone to hide her shape under baggy sweaters and to scrape her hair back in a rubber band. For never a day had seemed to go by without her stepbrother making a pass at her.

To say anything about it to her mother, after the most unhappy time she had endured, was something Mallon had found she just could not do. Though she had to admit that she'd come close that day Lee Jenkins came into her room just as she had finished dressing.

'Get out!' she screamed at him—a minute earlier and he would have caught her minus her blouse!

'Don't be like that,' he said in what he thought was his sexy voice, but which she found revolting, and, instead of leaving her room, he came further into it and, grabbing a hold of her, tried to kiss her.

She bit him—his language was colourful, but she cared not. Once he let her go and she was free of him, she wasn't hanging about.

She was badly shaken, and wanted to confide in her mother. But, somehow, protective of her still, Mallon could not tell her. Instead she took to propping a chair under the knob of her bedroom door at all times whenever she was in there on her own.

Then, horror of horrors, her mother had been married for only a year when her stepfather cast his lascivious glance on Mallon. At first she couldn't believe what her eyes and instincts were telling her. That was until the day he cornered her in the drawing room and, his eyes on her breasts, remarked, 'Little Mallon, you're not so little any more, I see.' Coming closer, his slack mouth all but slobbering, he demanded, 'Got a kiss for your stepdaddy?'

She was revolted, and told him truthfully, 'I'm going to be sick!'

She *was* sick, and later sat on her bed and cried, because she knew now, more than ever, that she could not tell her mother. Her parent would be destroyed.

Mallon sorely wanted to leave home. It wasn't home any more anyway. But money, which she had never had to particularly think of before, had been tight for some while. She knew that her father had left them well provided for, but only a few days ago her mother had suggested she might like to take a Saturday job, and Mallon had asked if they were having some temporary financial problem. Her mother had replied, 'I'm afraid it isn't temporary, Mallon, it's permanent,' and had looked so dreadfully unhappy Mallon had been unable to bear it.

She knew without having to ask where all the money had gone. Ambrose Jenkins had been spending freely, too freely, the money her father had invested. Incredibly, there was little of it remaining.

Lee Jenkins was as work-shy as his father, and had to be a constant drain on what resources her mother had remaining. Determined not to be a drain on those resources herself, Mallon left school and got herself a job.

As jobs went it wasn't much: a clerical assistant in a large and busy office. But, for her age, it didn't pay too badly. Though it wasn't sufficient to pay rent as well as keep her should she attempt the enormous step she wished to take and leave home.

The following two years dragged miserably by, and when she saw how badly her mother's marriage was faring, Mallon was glad she had not left home. Her mother started to realise what a dreadful mistake she had made in marrying Ambrose Jenkins, but did not seem to have the strength to do anything about his by then quite blatant philandering ways. Mallon knew her mother was suffering. But, feeling powerless to do anything about it, Mallon wanted to be there to support her when she finally did cry Enough!

While Mallon was doing everything she could to cold-shoulder both father and son without her mother being aware—which would only make her even more wretched—it was not her stepfather's habit of staying out nights and weekends, and coming home only to be fed and laundered, that brought things to a head. But money.

Both the Jenkins men were out that Wednesday when Mallon came home from work and found her mother in tears. 'Oh, darling!' Mallon cried, going over to her. 'What's the matter?'

Plenty, she learned in the next five minutes. Ambrose and her mother were splitting up, but that, it seemed, was not the reason for her mother's despair. But, as she explained, because she had foolishly listened to Ambrose Jenkins eighteen months ago when as near penury as made no difference, he had told her of a business venture that would almost immediately earn them double. It would, however, mean a quite substantial investment.

Evelyn Jenkins was not used to working with money, she had never needed to. But, aware that something needed to be done to get them solvent once more, she had been persuaded to borrow, using their lovely home as collateral.

It had all ended in tears. The upshot being that now, eighteen months later, the business venture had folded. With no more money forthcoming, Ambrose was leaving, and even the house no longer belonged to her mother.

'We've got to leave here,' her mother wept. 'This lovely house your father bought for us!'

Oddly then, though maybe because having reached rock bottom the only way was up, and perhaps aided by thinking of her gentleman former husband, Evelyn Jenkins seemed to gather some strength. Mallon could only guess at the inner torment her parent must have been through before she had confided in her. But the next morning, before Mallon could say she intended to take the day off work and start to look for somewhere to rent, her mother was telling her how she intended to contact a firm of lawyers that day to see if there was anything to be done.

Mallon hurried home that night to hear that John Frost, the head of the firm her father had always used, and who knew the family, had initially dealt personally with her mother. After a detailed check of all the paperwork he had passed the opinion that she had been criminally advised, had put a doubt on the fact that the money had been invested anywhere but in Ambrose Jenkins pocket, and had concluded that Evelyn Jenkins had a case for suing him.

Since, however, that man appeared to not have any money, there seemed no point whatsoever in taking that route. 'I think I would rather divorce him,' she decided. Mallon could only applaud her decision.

There followed months and months of upset. Ambrose wanted to behave like a single man, but didn't want to be divorced, apparently, and so was as obstructive as he knew how to be; which was considerably.

Although divorce was not John Frost's speciality, and he had handed the case over to someone whose subject it was, John Frost was always there to smile and encourage when her mother went to his offices to pursue the matter of the protracted proceedings.

Mallon and her mother moved into a tiny flat, the rent of which took quite a chunk out of Mallon's salary. She was not complaining— it was a joy not to have to live under the same roof as the Jenkins duo. A joy not to have to continually be on her guard against the loose-moralled, lascivious pair.

Her mother's divorce was finalised on Mallon's twentieth birthday. John Frost, by now something of a friend, took them to dinner to celebrate.

Finances were extremely tight and her mother did try to support herself, but she had never had to work outside of the home, and it was all too apparent that she neither enjoyed nor was cut out to stand in a shop serving all day, or to sit in an office trying to get to grips with a computer. Mallon couldn't bear it—her father would have been utterly distraught that life should have treated his beloved Evelyn this way.

'You don't have to go out to work, you know,' Mallon insisted. 'We can manage.'

Her mother looked uncertain. 'I have to contribute something. It isn't fair...'

'You do contribute. You're a wonderful homemaker.'

'But...' Evelyn Jenkins tried to argue, but Mallon could see that her heart wasn't in it. And eventually, with Mallon using every persuasion she could think of, her mother gave in—and for about eighteen months more they limped along on Mallon's salary.

Then suddenly everything started to improve. Mallon and her mother went out to dine with widower John Frost a few times, and invited him to their small flat in return. It didn't take much for Mallon to see that John was keen on her mother, and Mallon liked how protective he was with her.

The next time he asked the two of them to dine with him Mallon found a convenient 'work' excuse at the last minute, and left it to John Frost to persuade her mother that he would be equally delighted to take her out without her daughter.

On the work front matters were looking up too. Mallon had made steady progress and was rewarded with promotion to another department. With the move came a very welcome raise in salary which meant that she and her mother could begin to renew the odd item here and there that had worn out. While not riches—they still had nothing in the bank—her pay rise made life just that little bit easier.

With her move to a new department Mallon met two people she would be working with. Natasha Wallace, a pleasant if plain girl of about her own almost twenty-two years, and Keith Morgan who was three years older.

Mallon became friends with both of them. And, with John Frost and her mother seeing just a little more of each other—John taking care not to rush Evelyn—Mallon started to go out and about with Natasha; sometimes Keith would go with them.

Mallon had been well and truly put off men by the behaviour of Ambrose and Lee Jenkins, and while it did not particularly bother her she just could not see herself entering into any kind of a relationship with any man.

Which was why it came as something of a surprise to her that, four months into her friendship with Natasha and Keith, she began to realise that she had some quite warm feelings for Keith. Feelings which, to her further surprise and pleasure, she discovered were returned.

They did not always go out as a threesome. When Natasha started to put in some extra practice for a violin exam she was about to take, Keith and Mallon went out more and more as a twosome.

Even now as she lay wide awake in Harris Quillian's bed Mallon felt sick in her stomach as she recalled how, only three months ago, their feelings for each other starting to take over, she had been on the brink of committing herself to a very intimate relationship with Keith Morgan.

It had started on a Saturday when Natasha had been busy with her music and Mallon and Keith had been to the cinema. Keith had been kissing Mallon goodnight when he'd suddenly begged her to go away with him. 'I want to go to bed with you—you must want the same,' he urged. Oh, help—it was such a big step! 'You know you want me as much as I want you.'

She said no, but week after week for the next two months he again and again urged her to go away with him. Then one Saturday he told her he loved her. It was what she needed to hear.

She agreed, albeit, it was with a rather shaky 'Y-yes,' that she answered.

Keith didn't waste any time and told her on Monday that he had arranged their romantic tryst for the coming weekend, and would pick her up from her home on Saturday morning.

Why couldn't she tell her mother? Her mother had met both Keith and Natasha and would have understood. Mallon later wondered—could it be that at heart she had known that something was not quite right? But just then she managed to convince herself that, after the dreadful years her mother had endured, and with everything going so right for her just now—she seemed to be spending more and more time with John Frost—she did not want to give her parent the smallest cause to worry about her.

Mallon made her way home from work on Friday and made up her mind to tell her mother that night. For heaven's sake, Keith would be calling for her in the morning!

Her mother wasn't in but had left a note saying that John had phoned and had particularly wanted to discuss something with her, so could she meet him later that afternoon? She didn't think she would be late back.

Mallon hoped not. She was on edge, and knew that feeling wouldn't go away until she had told her mother her plans. When each hour ticked away and her mother didn't appear, Mallon guessed that John had taken her mother to dinner.

Which proved correct when, just after ten, John Frost brought her mother home. 'Um—we've got something to tell you,' Evelyn Jenkins said, but didn't have to—Mallon could see the joy they shared with each other.

'We're going to be married,' John could hardly wait to tell her. 'Is that all right with you, Mallon?'

She hadn't seen her mother looking so happy in years. 'You know it is!' Mallon beamed, and forgot all about Keith Morgan when she went over and the threesome embraced.

John had brought some champagne in with him and they talked for an age as the newly engaged couple shared with Mallon that they had steadily got to know each other over the years, and saw not one single reason to wait. They would marry next month and Mallon would give up the flat.

'Give up the flat?'

'Your mother will be moving into my home, Mallon,' John answered. 'It's my wish that you move into my home too.'

'Thank you,' she answered, not wanting to blight this happy time for them. But she somehow knew, much as she liked John and much as she would miss her mother dreadfully, that her place was not in her mother's new home. This, after all she'd been through, was a special time for her mother.

'That's settled, then.' John smiled, and went on to outline how he'd telephoned his married daughter in Scotland and she was flying down tomorrow for a family celebration dinner.

'Oh!' Mallon exclaimed. Oh, grief, she had forgotten all about Keith Morgan!

'Don't say you can't make it, darling. Did you have some other arrangement?'

'Keith—er...'

'I'm sure he'll understand. This is a family occasion, after all.' Evelyn Jenkins beamed.

'Of course. I'll give him a ring,' Mallon said with a smile and realised, perhaps because of her mother's lovely news, that she didn't feel unduly upset that her weekend with Keith was off.

He did not understand when she rang him. Instead, he was furious. 'I've booked the hotel!' he protested angrily. 'Your mother's been married before—what's so special now?' If he couldn't see, Mallon wasn't about to try and explain.

'I'm sorry,' she apologised. 'I'll see you on Monday.'

The celebratory dinner went wonderfully well. John's daughter, Isobel, was as thrilled as Mallon that the two had finally decided to marry.

By Monday, feeling uncomfortable that she had let Keith down, Mallon went to seek him out to apologise again and to try and make him see how important it had been to her mother that she had been there.

'Keith,' she began, going over to his desk.

'Mallon, I...' he said at the same time, for no reason she could think of, looking almost sheepish.

''Morning, Keith!' They both turned to see Natasha standing there, looking more animated than Mallon had ever seen her. Natasha grinned at them both but addressed Keith when she said, 'I thought you'd like to know I didn't get into trouble when I got in last night.'

Mallon stared at her, and then smiled. What was more natural? She had let Keith down and Natasha was an old chum. 'You were out with Keith last night?' she commented, still feeling a touch uncomfortable, but glad that Keith hadn't had a totally dull weekend. Though... Suddenly some instinct in Mallon started to quiver. She knew *she* was feeling uncomfortable, but what the Dickens was Keith looking so uncomfortable about? 'You've been out with Keith on a Sunday before,' Mallon commented slowly. 'What was so different about last night?'

Keith found his shoes worthy of inspection, while Natasha answered, 'Only the fact that I didn't go home at all on Saturday night.'

Something inside Mallon froze. 'Now that is different.' Somehow she managed to make her tone light. 'You went away with Keith?' she asked, a very personal question she knew, but she needed some answers here.

Natasha's eyes sparkled. 'It was wonderful, wasn't it, Keith?' He didn't answer.

There was only one other question which, in normal times, Mallon would not have dreamed of asking. 'Did you sleep together?' she asked, her light tone gone.

Natasha looked a shade put out but, possibly because of their past friendship, answered honestly, if a shade coolly, 'We did. That was rather the whole point of going.'

Mallon looked at Keith. He did not deny it. 'We'd better get on with some work.' She left them and went to her desk. She was deaf to Keith Morgan's entreaties when he explained he had been so very angry with her for letting him down, but that it was her, Mallon, that he loved.

Mallon knew then that she was at a crossroads in her life. She no longer wanted to work in the same department with Keith and Natasha. She felt deeply, instinctively, that she should not live with her mother and John Frost when they married, but knew if she insisted on staying on in the flat alone that her mother would be upset. And she had endured more than enough upset already.

Over the next few days Mallon figured it out. She still wasn't any happier working with Natasha and Keith—but no one was going to know it. What she needed, Mallon decided, was a clean break, a new job, a...

Suddenly she had it. The only excuse her mother was likely to accept for her not moving in with her and John would be if she said she had applied for a job in another area.

Mallon looked at the state of her finances. She wanted to treat her mother to a really lovely outfit to be married in. More genius arrived. How about if she found a live-in job? Brilliant! She could then spend her final month's salary on something really gorgeous for her mother. And living in, board and lodgings obviously taken care of, she could limp along quite well on any money left over until pay day.

Mallon got out of Harris Quillian's bed, musing how she had thought everything through. Then, opting for the job advertised for housekeeper, clerical background an advantage, in preference to one for a hotel receptionist because of her lack of training in that area, she had acted. Had *she* made a mistake! She had still been feeling very much let down by Keith Morgan's behaviour when, on top of it, she had met that reptile Roland Phillips. Grief, was she ever off men—permanently!

Mallon went to one of the bedroom windows and stared out. The rain had stopped, thank goodness. If it stayed dry perhaps the roofers could come and take a look at… Harris Quillian had been kind, she suddenly found herself thinking. When she came to think about it, more than kind. Her mother would have been overwrought had Harris given her a lift to her mother's new home.

She had a lot to thank him for, Mallon knew. Not least his generosity in giving her all that money. Salary, he'd called it. But he had trusted her not to do a flit at the first opportunity. Though, from his point of view, he could afford to trust her not to run off with the family silver. She turned to look back into the uncarpeted room, and found she was smiling— there was hardly anything worth pinching.

Mallon decided to investigate the water heating system. She had been weary enough last night and had endured sufficient water on her body from her drenching to think it wouldn't matter if she went to bed without first showering. But it wouldn't surprise her to find that brand-new shower in the bathroom was not yet functional.

It was functional, she discovered, and she had a lovely time standing under the warm-to-hot spray. Harris Quillian thought she had a beautiful face and a superb figure, she found herself idly musing—and abruptly stepped out from the shower. For goodness' sake—as if she cared!

Not that there had been anything 'personal' in his remarks. She put his comments from her—she was sure he'd had a heavy date last night. No doubt with some luscious sophisticate. He certainly wasn't the least bit personally interested in the likes of one Mallon Braithwaite. He couldn't have made it plainer that he wanted the place to himself at weekends. Which, she sighed, unsmiling, couldn't suit her better.

She had unlocked the front and rear doors and was investigating the refrigerator, glad to see that Faye Phillips had stocked her brother up with cartons and cartons of the sort of milk that kept for months, when Mallon heard the first of the builders arrive.

Shortly afterwards there was a knock at the kitchen door. 'Miss Braithwaite? It's my firm that's doing the rebuilding. I'm Bob Miller,' he introduced himself. 'Mr Quillian's been on to us. We had a bit of rain yesterday, didn't we?' he understated.

She took to Bob Miller, a muscly sort of man of about fifty. He didn't seem to question who she was or why she was there, but just accepted it. 'You could say that,' she agreed.

'All right if I come in and take a look at the ceiling that came down yesterday?'

'Of course. Er…' She remembered Harris's remark yesterday about keeping an army of builders supplied with tea and coffee. 'Shall I make some tea?'

Bob gave her a wide grin. 'Now that's the way to start the week,' he accepted.

It was a busy week too. Had she at any time wondered what she would do all day, then she had no difficulty in filling those hours. Throughout the week she met Cyril, the carpenter, who as well as doing his other work fitted locks on two bedroom doors and put security catches on all bedroom windows. She also met Charlie, Dean, Baz and Ron, who were excellent with plumbing stonework, and electrics. And Ken, who was something of an intellectual, and who liked working out in the open air. There was Del too, who had a lovely tenor voice, and who sang throughout most of the day. And lastly Kevin, the 'gofer'.

It was Kevin who gave her a lift in 'the van' when he had to visit the building suppliers in town. 'Take as long as you like,' he offered cheerfully as he dropped her off at the super-market. 'I'll be ages.'

Mallon purchased fresh fruit and vegetables and other provisions, and also bought a news-paper, plus stationery and postage stamps. She studied the situations vacant column when she got back, but there was little there of interest to her. Still, Harris had suggested that the builders would be there for three months, so there was no particular hurry. And anyway, this time, she didn't want to rush into the first likely job she saw.

Apart from the bed Harris had promised, several other items of furniture arrived that week. Mallon directed the sofa and one of the padded chairs to the drawing room, which was, as yet, like the bedrooms uncurtained and un-

carpeted. The wardrobe, desk and another padded chair were carried up to her room, and,
since she more or less lived in the kitchen, she
had another easy chair put in there.

She found that as well as thinking frequently
of her mother and John Frost, and trying not
to think of the likes of Keith Morgan and
Roland Phillips, she thought a good deal of
Harris Quillian too.

Contrary to his comment about her incubating pneumonia, she had not so much as
sneezed. In fact, given that she was still having
the most ghastly dreams, and had once or
twice had to leave her bed to go and sit in the
safe haven of the kitchen until she was more
at peace, she had never felt better.

Would Harris really have driven her to a police station to report his brother-in-law for assault? she wondered. But, since his sister was
apparently hoping to go back to her husband
once their trial separation was over, Mallon
thought it doubtful.

Harris had said he might come down on
Friday, so on Friday morning Mallon packed
a bag ready to move out for the weekend, then
went in search of Kevin. He was frequently

trundling off in the van to a village shop two miles up the road 'for the lads'.

'Would you give me a lift the next time you're going to Sherwins?' she asked him.

'Pleased to,' he answered in his cheery way. And twenty minutes later came to the kitchen door looking for her.

She made various purchases at Sherwins, who seemed to keep a supply of absolutely everything, and by that evening there was a vase of flowers standing in the hearth, and, with a few rugs scattered about, the drawing room was looking quite homey.

But Harris Quillian did not appear, and Mallon went to bed that night aware of the oddest pang of disappointment. She immediately scoffed at any such notion—but slept badly.

She was glad to leave her bed on Saturday morning. Bob Miller had said his men would be working that morning. Mallon showered and dressed in jeans and a tee shirt and went downstairs to get busy.

One of the men had brought her a bag of plums. By midday she had two plum pies made, and was just thinking of making a batch of cakes—they'd be gone in seconds, she knew, but they were a good-hearted bunch of men—when, glancing to the kitchen window, she saw a car glide by with Harris at the wheel.

She hadn't expected to see him until at the earliest next Friday now. Suddenly she was smiling—only then did she realise that she was pleased to see him.

CHAPTER THREE

MALLON heard Harris coming along the hall, and unexpectedly felt ridiculously shy all at once. He was as she remembered him when, tall, broad-shouldered and steady-eyed, he came into the kitchen.

She felt oddly tongue-tied, and he did not speak straight away, but stood in the doorway just looking at her, as if it was the first time he had seen her. Only then did it dawn on her, as his glance went over her gleaming blonde head and down over her tee shirt and denim-covered long legs, that this was the first time he had seen her with her hair looking anything other than soaking wet or dry and in a tangle.

'I polish up quite well,' she said in a rush, feeling self-conscious suddenly. It was the first time too that he had seen her with her nose powdered and wearing dry clothes that were her own.

She tensed as soon as the words were out, realising she might have invited a personal remark. He smiled, disarmingly, and she had an idea he knew she wished she had kept silent.

Any feeling of tension swiftly disappeared, though, when the closest he got to a personal remark was to say, 'I was going to take my bag upstairs, but I couldn't resist the smell of home baking.'

She felt self-conscious again. For goodness' sake, pull yourself together. 'Del brought me a bag of plums,' she found herself answering, and could have groaned at how stupid she felt she sounded. 'He's a plasterer.' She found she couldn't shut up. 'There are a few buckets and bowls on the landing in case we have another cloudburst,' she gabbled on. 'One part of the roof has been repaired, but there are a few fresh leaks, and the roofer-tiling man can't get here before Monday.' Stop it! Stop it! 'Would you like a coffee?' she changed tack to ask abruptly—and instantly felt her sudden change of tone to almost snappy might have offended him.

But no. 'I'd love one,' he replied. 'I'll just take my bag up, and you can fill me in on anything I need to know.'

She was glad to see him go; it gave her a chance to get herself back together again.

Good grief, what was the matter with her? She had never felt shy or tongue-tied in a man's company before! Tongue-tied? It sounded like it, the way she had rattled away! Was it nerves? Surely her experience with Roland Phillips hadn't shattered her confidence to that extent! She most earnestly hoped not, though acknowledged she had previously received a few wounds from her experiences with men like her ex-stepfather and his son, not to mention the faithless Keith Morgan. She probably still nursed a few non-physical scars, without taking on any more from Harris's brother-in-law.

Mallon had the coffee made when Harris came back into the kitchen, and thought she had herself all of one piece again—until he observed casually, 'I see the bed has arrived.'

'You've been in my room?' she questioned, at once hostile.

His casual demeanour vanished. 'I'm not allowed to check my instructions with regard to windows and doors have been carried out?' he questioned, a shade toughly.

Mallon looked from him and into her coffee. What was wrong with her? It was his house;

he could do what he jolly well pleased. Silence between them stretched.

Then, his tough tone gone, 'You're upset,' he commented mildly.

She looked up. 'You make me sound like some touchy diva. I'm sorry,' she apologised, and tried to explain. 'I just—like my privacy.' She had no intention of explaining further that it had begun years ago, when she'd had to prop a chair under the knob of her bedroom door to keep would-be intruders out.

'You're a strange mixture,' Harris offered pleasantly.

She didn't thank him for it. 'I'm supposed to ask how?'

Her belligerence didn't touch him. 'You welcome me with the smell of home cooking—then give me the cross-and-garlic treatment in case I get the wrong idea.'

Nothing escaped him, she saw, but didn't care for his summing up. 'The cooking wasn't for you in particular, even if you are welcome to it,' she retorted, and had suddenly had enough. 'I've a bag packed. I'll go.'

'Where?' he asked in surprise, his expression hardening. 'You're not leaving just because...'

'I'm not *leaving* leaving. I'm going to a ho-tel overnight,' she explained. 'You said… You've forgotten!' she accused.

'No, I haven't,' he denied. 'I just thought, on account of our—scratchy—start, that you were not intending to come back.' Again his tone altered. 'You're welcome to stay if you want…' he began.

'I don't want!' she cut in bluntly.

'Pardon me for mentioning it,' he retorted pithily. 'Forgive me for feeling guilty that I appear to be turning you out,' he added curtly.

Mallon didn't want to apologise, didn't want to be always in the wrong—and that was how this man made her feel. Without looking at him, without bothering to finish her coffee, she marched stiff-backed out from the kitchen and up to her room.

It took but a few seconds to collect the bag she had packed and in no time she was on her way back down the stairs again. By the time she had reached the hall, however, Harris Quillian had come out from the kitchen and was standing there, car keys in hand. When she neared him he stretched out a hand for her overnight bag.

'I was going to ask Kevin if he could drive me into town,' she said, hanging on to her bag. 'He very often goes for building supplies and things they're short of.'

'I'll take you,' Harris answered evenly, and before she could marshal up any sort of an argument he had taken her overnight bag, and she was seated beside him in his car and they were driving out between the stone gateposts of Harcourt House.

Why, though, did she want to argue? Mallon found she was silently questioning. Harris had been nothing but kind and decent to her. Suddenly she felt quite dreadful, and, 'I'm sorry,' she blurted out, and when he momentarily took his eyes off the road to glance at her, she went on, 'I don't know why I'm so...' she searched for a word, and used his; it seemed to serve for how she felt '...so scratchy.'

'I do,' he surprised her by answering, his eyes once more on the road up ahead, his tone mild.

Mallon stared at his profile. 'You do?'

'Could it be you're still suffering with some trauma from what happened to you last Sunday?'

Mallon thought about it. That soaking as she'd sped and then trudged through the torrential rain had been traumatic enough without all that had gone before. All this week she had experienced horrendous flashbacks of Roland Phillips's lust-filled face as he'd tried to tear her clothes from her. It came to her then that it was unlikely that anyone would recover instantly from something like that.

'You could be right,' she conceded thoughtfully, but, not wanting to stress the point, felt she should admit, 'I have been having flashbacks and the most awful dreams.'

'You've not been sleeping well?'

'It's not as if I have to get up to go to work in the morning,' she answered lightly.

'According to Bob Miller, when I spoke with him Thursday, you're always up and about and have the kettle boiling when he arrives at seven forty-five,' Harris drawled.

He'd got her there. 'I didn't know you'd got your spies about!'

'Have you gone all scratchy again?' Harris asked, but it wasn't annoyance she heard in his voice, but teasing. She found she liked his teasing.

'I shan't say sorry again,' she told him with a smile. But was serious when she went on, 'For all you've been so kind, you…'

'Hey, you'll be giving me a halo next!'

'I doubt you're that saintly. But it was…good of you to stop last Sunday the way you did.'

'Water under the bridge. The main thing now is to see if there's anything to be done about those flashbacks and dreams. Would you see someone professional? I can arrange…'

'Heavens, that's not necessary! I wouldn't have told you if I'd thought you'd take it so seriously!'

'It is serious, Mallon. You're on edge with me a lot of the time. I don't want you to end up afraid of men because of what my brother-in-law tried to do to…'

'For goodness' sake!' she exclaimed irritably. 'I'm not afraid of men! I'm chatting to one or other of the builders all day!' she went on indignantly. And, when Harris Quillian didn't interrupt, she found she was storming on, 'I might be a bit cautious sometimes, a touch watchful, but that's not all down to Roland Phillips, as ghastly as…' She broke off, hating Quillian again that he had made her angry enough to be heedless of what she was saying.

And hated him some more when it became clear he wasn't going to pretend he hadn't heard what she had just said. 'You've had a similar experience?' he questioned harshly. Turning sharply to look at her. 'That makes Phillips's actions doubly heinous!' he gritted.

'I don't want to talk about it. And it was nothing nearly as bad, anyway,' she answered snappily. 'Watch where you're going,' she ordered bossily. 'In fact...' she went on when she could see that they had arrived in the main street in town '...you can drop me off here and I'll...'

He ignored her—and she wanted to thump him. Never had she met such a man. She wanted to find her own hotel. A bed and breakfast place in her view would be just ideal. But, no, he had to take her to the smartest hotel in town!

When he halted the car in the car park of the Clifton Hotel, Mallon was determined she was not going to go in. She looked stonily at him—he looked stonily back. 'Don't give me a hard time, Mallon,' he said—a shade wearily, she thought, and all at once she felt dreadful. Without question he must work hard and put in long hours to be the success everything about him spoke of him being, and had probably left London for Upper Macey and Harcourt House with the hope of being able to unwind for some hours before he went back into the cut and thrust of his financial world again.

'I'm...' She opened her mouth to say she was sorry, then was unsure why she wanted to apologise, so said instead, 'It looks a bit plush. How do you think the jeans and tee shirt will go down?'

Suddenly warm grey eyes were smiling into wide deeply blue eyes. 'You're a snob, Mallon Braithwaite,' he teased.

'I'm not,' she denied, adding, deliberately ungrammatically, 'I've just been brought up proper.'

He started to grin, her heart gave the most unexpected thump, and she looked quickly away. She found the door catch, and by the time Harris had taken up her overnight bag and was coming round to her, she was out of the car.

He had obviously used the Clifton Hotel as his base in the initial stages of negotiating the purchase of Harcourt House and subsequent on-site meetings with architects and planners, Mallon gathered. Because he was greeted by name and it seemed as though nothing would be any trouble for him.

In no time she found she was booked into the busy hotel and Harris was standing looking down at her. 'I'll come and collect you tomorrow,' he said, and she felt guilty at putting him to so much bother.

'I'll get a taxi back,' she insisted.

'Are you casting aspersions on my driving?'

She smiled; it turned into a laugh. 'I wouldn't dare,' she replied, and felt secure, and continued to feel so even when his glance strayed to her upward-curving mouth.

After he had gone Mallon felt strange, not bereft exactly, and couldn't put her finger on quite how she felt; but she missed him.

Up in her hotel room she scorned such non-sense. She was just feeling a bit cut adrift that was all. She didn't know anyone here and, well, her life had changed fairly dramatically recently. Apart from changing her job and parting with a boyfriend she had, until not so many weeks ago, always lived with her mother.

Thinking of her parent, Mallon picked up the telephone. Her mother had rung her at Almora Lodge ten days ago, so she had better call in case her parent thought to phone Almora Lodge again.

She had rung not a moment too soon, Mallon discovered, when her mother heard her voice. 'I was going to ring you!' the new Mrs Frost exclaimed, sounding well, extremely happy, and pleased to hear her.

'Everything all right with you?' Mallon asked.

'Couldn't be better. John's such a love. I'd quite forgotten how true gentlemen behave,' Evelyn Frost confided, and Mallon, her emotions welling up, felt choked. Those dreadful years her mother had endured when living with Ambrose Jenkins must have been truly awful. 'How are things with you?' her mother asked. 'Have you seen much of your employer this week?' She meant Roland Phillips, Mallon knew, having told her during their last telephone conversation that he was seldom home.

'I haven't seen him since last Sunday,' Mallon answered, finding it totally beyond her to blight her mother's new-found happiness— she would be fearfully upset if she knew even the barest details of her running away from Roland Phillips. She would be equally upset, and would probably insist she came home straight away to live with her and John, should Mallon tell her the whole of it and how she came to have a new employer.

Mallon had a long chat with her parent and finally replaced the phone, growing even more convinced that her mother had done the right thing in marrying John Frost—Ambrose Jenkins didn't bear comparison.

Aware that the charge for staying overnight in the Clifton Hotel was going to make quite a hole in her finances, Mallon opted to go out and buy a sandwich for her lunch. She had a look around the shops while she was out, and popped into a supermarket for some flour and a few other odds and ends.

She was back in her room well before it was time for dinner and had thought she might go out for a snack somewhere. Then found she was wondering what Harris was having to eat. She hoped he was helping himself to the plum pie—and realised she was thinking of him with some affection.

Good grief! She barely knew the man! True, he had been more than kind. But, anyway, he was probably far from starving. He had a car; if he didn't fancy cooking for himself, he could always drive into town for dinner.

Maybe he would come to the Clifton Hotel for a meal. That settled it; she *would* go out. Perhaps, though, he had a lady-friend locally; he was footloose and fancy-free after all.

All at once Mallon was feeling restless. Blow him. The hotel's dining room would be big enough for both of them. She had earlier unpacked her overnight bag. She went over to the wardrobe and took out the smart trousers and top she had hung there.

The hotel dining room, when she went down, was fairly crowded, she observed. Apart from couples and foursomes there was one very large party, plainly celebrating something. But Harris Quillian was not there.

Mallon got on with the meal she had ordered, and by the time she was eating her pudding she had realised that the big party were a family party celebrating a golden wedding anniversary. She wasn't particularly looking in that direction, but could hardly miss the huge bouquets of flowers that were carried over to that table, or miss that the sprightly, if mature, couple—who didn't look anywhere near old enough to have been married for fifty years—standing together to cut the anniversary cake and to be photographed.

She opted to take her coffee in the hotel lounge and felt less restless on leaving the dining room than when she had entered, though found as she sipped her coffee that she was again thinking of Harris Quillian. The fact that, at around thirty-five years or so, he was unmarried spoke of some pretty fleet footwork, she decided, and again found she was wondering if there was some female locally who had tipped his decision to purchase the Upper Macey property. On reflection, she thought not. If he was quite content with his bachelor status, thank you, he was hardly likely to put it in jeopardy by having anything remotely suggesting a 'steady' woman-friend locally.

'Is this seat taken?'

She looked up to see a pleasant man of about twenty-five had come on a hunt for spare chairs. 'Please take it,' she said with a smile, and discovered that he was in no hurry to dash away, until someone needing the chair reminded him of his duty.

Ten minutes later Mallon was thinking of returning to her room when the man came back. By that time there was another chair free close by. She thought he was going to take it over to his party, but he instead brought it to where she was sitting.

'Have you any objection if I sit here for a few minutes?' he asked. 'Just say, and I'll go.'

He seemed harmless enough, and it wasn't as if she was in the room on her own. His party were but yards away on the other side of the room. 'Won't your companions be expecting you back?'

'It's my grandparents' golden wedding,' he replied, and explained, 'All the family are taking a trip down memory lane.' He smiled. 'I'm not old enough for such goings on.'

Over the next twenty minutes Mallon got to quite like Tony Wilson. He was pleasant without being pushy, lived and worked about eight miles away, and had opted to stay overnight in the hotel with his family. Mallon saw no reason not to be as open as him when he asked if she was on holiday in the area, and told him that she was only there overnight.

'What sort of work do you do?' he wanted to know.

'I'm doing a temporary house-sitting job at the moment,' she felt able to tell him, explaining, 'There are deliveries and builders, things like that.'

'The owners are away most of the time?' Tony queried.

'The owner came home this morning,' Mallon answered.

'And gave you the weekend off,' Tony accepted.

Mallon thought it was time she went and made her acquaintance with the paperback thriller she had purchased in the supermarket. 'Some of your family are looking over this way. I think your presence is required.'

Tony glanced back to where someone so like him he had to be his father had his eyes on him. Tony waved, and, turning back to her, invited, 'Come with me. Come and join the party.'

'Wouldn't dream of it,' she answered, the idea of gate-crashing a special golden wedding celebration unthinkable.

'They'd love you to.'

She shook her head, almost said she had a good book waiting, then realised that might sound rude. 'No, but thank you,' she said, and smiled because he was nice.

Her book didn't live up to its blurb, or perhaps it was that she was suddenly feeling restless again. Having tried without success to get into it, Mallon put her book down and went and had a long soak in the bath, letting her mind wander until it all at once struck her that for most of the time she had been thinking of Harris Quillian.

True, he had been kind to her, more than kind to her. Generous too, insisting on paying her wages in advance the way he had. But, remembering that he had been more than sharp with her on occasions, she decided that he did not deserve so much attention in her head.

More bad dreams invaded her sleep that night and Mallon awoke glad to leave her bed. She showered and dressed, exchanging yesterday's white tee shirt for a fresh one, observing from the grey skies that it looked as though they were going to pay today for yesterday's sunshine.

The threatening rain arrived, in torrents, while she was in the dining room having her breakfast. Did roofers work in the rain? she wondered, and hoped so, otherwise, if this kept up, she would be spending much of her time tomorrow emptying buckets and bowls.

She smiled at the thought, and realised, quite crazily, she fully admitted, that for all the plushness of this hotel she was ready to go back to Harcourt House. In fact, for all its far from finished state, she was actually looking forward to returning. Whoa, there, she instructed herself, now don't start getting attached to the place. In three months' time—sooner if the right job came up—she would be leaving.

She was in a thoughtful mood as she left the dining room. She had no idea why Harcourt House should have any effect on her at all. With the exception of a few of the rooms most of the place was in a mess. If the electricians weren't cutting off the power for some reason or other, then the plumbers were cutting off the water while they worked on whatever new problem had presented itself. And that was without the constant banging and crashing of work in general as the builders went about their business. And yet, when she cared more for peace and quiet than all the hammering and hollering that went on, Mallon owned she sometimes came near to feeling quite tranquil in Harris Quillian's home.

She went to her room and packed her few belongings but, unsure what time Harris would come for her, she left her bag in her room while she went down to Reception to pay for the hotel's services.

'The account is settled,' the receptionist informed her when she asked for her bill.

'Settled? There must be some mistake. I...'

'Mr Quillian left instructions for the account to be sent to him.' The receptionist smiled. 'I wouldn't dare hand it over to you.'

Mallon was just about to inform her that she would jolly well have to when Tony Wilson came up to her, and the receptionist turned to deal with someone else.

'I was hoping I'd see you this morning,' he said frankly, and as someone else came up to the reception desk they moved a few steps out of the way. 'You went off in such a rush last night, I didn't get chance to ask if perhaps you might like to come out with me one evening? We could have dinner somewhere if...'

'I'm sorry, Tony.' She stopped him right there. As nice as he was, it would be a very long time before she so much as considered going out with anyone again. But, because he was so nice, and had such an open way with him, she tried to be honest too as she told him, 'I've only recently broken up with someone—I'm not ready to date again yet.'

'Oh, I'm sorry,' Tony replied, but wasn't ready to give up. 'Perhaps if you gave me your phone number we could talk on the phone? Get to know each other a little. You could get to know me...'

'No,' she interrupted him, and he could see that she meant it.

But he still wasn't giving up. 'Will you be here in this hotel next weekend?' he wanted to know—and Mallon just had to laugh.

And at that point she all at once became aware that they had company. She half turned. Severe grey eyes were boring into her. 'Harris!' she exclaimed in surprise. She hadn't seen him come in, hadn't heard him approach, and in actual fact hadn't expected him to be at the hotel so early.

He did not, she rather thought, look exactly delirious to be there. Tony hadn't moved, and Harris, having switched his gaze to him, was not saying a word but was just standing there looking at him. She realised she had no choice.

'Tony, this is—my employer, Harris Quillian. Harris, Tony Wilson,' she completed, and stood by while the two civilly acknowledged each other.

Then Harris was bluntly asking, 'If you're ready?' and Mallon again felt the urge to thump him.

'I'll just pop up and get my bag,' she said politely, and had Tony Wilson for an escort to the hotel lifts.

'You're sure about that phone number?' he pressed as they stood waiting for the lift to arrive.

'Positive,' she answered, and glanced over to see that Harris Quillian was staring unsmiling at the two of them. In direct contrast, and doubting she would ever see Tony Wilson again, she gave Tony her best smile.

She wasn't smiling as she went up in the lift, though. Okay, so Quillian was obviously in a hurry to get back to London, but it wasn't her fault that he'd had to come out of his way to collect her. She would have been more than happy to have returned by taxi. In fact she had said she would. So it was his fault, not hers.

Having established that fact, Mallon collected her overnight bag, gathered up the plastic carriers of her purchases of yesterday, and rode down in the lift. It annoyed her that he wasn't standing around waiting impatiently for her but was in conversation with the receptionist—who was all but drooling at his charm.

'Ready when you are,' Mallon interrupted brightly.

He turned, glanced at her shopping bearing the supermarket logo. Although he took her overnight bag from her, as he said goodbye to the receptionist so he seemed to say goodbye to most of his charm. Mallon decided she cared not, and walked ahead of him out of the hotel.

She anticipated a silent drive back to Harcourt House. For a while all that could be heard above the purr of the car's engine was the fast speed of the windscreen wipers as they dealt with the downpour. But then, in his unfriendliest tone yet, Quillian demanded to know, 'Who was that?'

'Who?' She knew full well whom he might mean but, while he might be in a rush to get back to London, she was not feeling very friendly either and was in no hurry to co-operate.

'Wilson!' he replied curtly.

'A fellow guest.'

'You met him yesterday?'

What *was* this? She decided she would not answer, but, on thinking about it, had to suppose there must be some point to this third degree. 'That's right,' she replied at last.

'You had dinner with him?'

'No.'

'But you've arranged to see him again.'

'No, I haven't!' she denied sharply.

'Where does he live?'

'Quite close.'

'You've told him where you live?'

'Am I likely to?' Mallon retorted heatedly. She'd had just about enough of this. Though, hang on a minute, perhaps the whole point of all this was that Quillian didn't want his address given out to all and sundry—or to any chance acquaintance. She could only suppose that as she liked her privacy, so did he like his.

Mallon had thought, her answer satisfactory, that Harris Quillian had finished with the subject. But she was proved wrong when, still in a demanding frame of mind apparently, he snarled, 'You've given him your phone number?'

It gave her great pleasure to be able to answer loftily, 'It may have escaped your notice, but we don't happen to have a telephone.'

Had she thought her lofty tone might annoy him, however, she discovered she was mistaken. In fact his voice had lost its harsh edge and was almost pleasant when he enquired, 'You don't have a mobile?'

'No,' she replied, and wished the journey to end so that he could clear off back to London.

A couple of minutes ticked by, then—and she was sure it wasn't to make amends for being so bossy with his questioning—Harris Quillian was observing, 'You've been shopping, I see.'

'I needed some flour and stuff,' she replied politely, if woodenly.

'I never thought of that. I shall have to let you have some housekeeping money.'

Honestly! This man! 'Are you deliberately trying to provoke me?' Mallon demanded crossly.

Harris turned to glance at her. 'What did I do?' he asked, and seemed genuinely not to know.

'It's enough that, besides all that money you gave me last week, you'll pay my hotel bill!' she flared.

'Ah!' he murmured. Then said softy, 'Proud Mallon, are you going to forgive me for treading on your sensitivities?'

Her anger went in a moment—she couldn't understand it. She had an urge to smile, and turned her head to look out of the side window just in case he was giving her another brief glance and caught her smiling.

But it was no good. Something was bubbling up inside of her, and she turned back to look at him. 'Why do I want to laugh?' she asked.

Harris glanced her way again, and after a moment's thought, suggested, 'Because basically, at root, you've a sunny temperament. Life recently, and I suspect not so recently, hasn't given you a happy time—your sunny side is only now starting to reassert itself.'

That slightly winded her. 'I didn't ask for in-depth psychoanalysis!' she offered stiffly, no longer feeling like laughing.

But he laughed. She felt miffed that he should. 'Was that what I did?' She didn't deign to answer. He was not a bit bothered, but went on, 'May I compliment you on what *you* did?'

That stirred her interest. 'What did I do?' she asked, puzzled.

'You've started to make Harcourt House look a little more like home.'

She stared at him, and, yes, felt a little flattered that he must have noticed she had changed the linen and put out clean towels. 'You've been in the drawing room?'

'The flowers were an added touch,' he confirmed, and suddenly all animosity between them seemed to have disappeared.

Mallon could not understand the warm glow she experienced to see Harcourt House again. Even in the rain the house seemed to welcome her. 'Have you time for coffee before you go?' she asked Harris as he carried her bags of groceries into the kitchen.

Placing the carriers down on the kitchen table, he looked over to her. 'I'm going somewhere?' he asked.

'You're...' She broke off—hadn't he, last Sunday, said something about collecting her from her hotel shortly before he went back to London again? Whatever, the unexpected surge of pleasure she felt that he was apparently meaning to stay around for a few hours more gave a hiding to her earlier wish that he would clear off back to London. 'I'll take my bag up,' she said, and headed for the door. Grief—she was *pleased* he was staying around!

Any wondering about what was going on that she should feel so pleased was abruptly abandoned when, on reaching the landing, she saw that the bowls she had yesterday strategically placed to catch any rain leaks were now full enough to be close to overflowing.

Dropping her bag where she stood, Mallon opened the door of the nearest, as yet unfinished room with an adjoining bathroom, and carefully picked up the nearest bowl. Because it was so full she had to carry it carefully, but once she had tipped the contents away into the bath she did a speedy turnabout to replace the bowl before the incessant dripping rain could do much damage.

She carried out the same procedure with the next bowl, going slowly while it was full. This time, though, when she swung about in her hurry to replace the bowl, she cannoned straight into Harris, who had obviously come up the stairs, assessed the situation, and was immediately lending a hand.

Unfortunately, while her bowl was empty, his was full. With Mallon going full pelt into him, Harris had small chance of depositing the entire contents of his bowl into the bath. With a great deal of speed and dexterity, a good half found its intended target while the remainder went over Mallon and the floor.

The water was cold and Mallon reeled back. But even as she gasped from the sudden shock of it, she would have laughed. Her mouth did begin to curve upwards. But then her eyes went to Harris, and she no longer felt like laughing. Because he wasn't looking at her face, but to where the water had tipped down the front of her.

Stunned, she followed his gaze and nearly gasped anew; her tee shirt, that had a few minutes ago been more than adequate cover, now clung to her like a second skin and was now revealing the full curves of her breasts and where the shock of cold water had made their tips stand out in hardened peaks. Harris Quillian was just standing there and staring at her breasts as if fascinated!

The bowl dropped from her hands, its clatter as it hit the floor bringing his eyes abruptly upwards to her shaken expression. 'Mallon,

I...' he began, but she wasn't waiting around to hear anything.

She pushed past him, taking to her heels, barely knowing where she was heading until she found herself in the sanctuary of her room.

But it wasn't a sanctuary, because Harris had followed her. 'Get out!' she yelled at him, alarm bells going off in her head, pictures haunting her—she'd screamed the same thing at Lee Jenkins all those years ago!

Harris's answer was to come swiftly up to her and take a firm grip on her upper arms. 'Calm down,' he instructed, and she tried to get free. 'I'm not going to hurt you. You're safe with me. Safe,' he repeated. 'Get that into your jumpy head. You're safe.'

Mallon stared at him. His grey eyes were holding hers firmly as he concentrated on making her believe him, that she was safe, that he would not hurt her. She ceased struggling, but was still watching him warily.

'Listen to me,' he continued, when he could see he had her full attention. 'Things like that happen. Fact. Anyone would have looked at you to see what damage had been done. Fact. You're distrustful, and I can see why. But try to trust that I just happen to be a male with...'

She'd had enough of being lectured. 'With eyes that can't help lingering,' she butted in antagonistically, and discovered that her words had more strength than any pushing and shoving she had done to get free of his grip.

A harsh glint came to his eyes, and abruptly he let go his hold on her. 'You're impossible to get through to like this!' he rapped, and, turning sharply about, he went striding from her room.

The next sound she heard was the purr of his car being driven down the drive. She went mutinously to the window and was in time to see Harris steering the vehicle through the stone pillars.

No doubt he had changed his mind about not rushing to return to London. Well, she was glad, glad, glad. With any luck he would forget to ever come back.

CHAPTER FOUR

MIRACULOUSLY the rain had ceased at some time during the night and Mallon awoke to a gloriously sunny morning. She wished she had awakened feeling as sunny. Harris had suggested that basically she had a sunny nature; nightmarish dreams during the night had clouded her morning.

She left her bed in a sombre frame of mind, her bad dreams not the only cloud on her day. Yesterday, because of her attitude, Harris had curtailed his visit. He had come down to unwind a little and she had put the kibosh on that.

Feeling very ashamed of herself, Mallon went over the events of yesterday that had led to Harris departing early. 'You're safe with me. Get that into your jumpy head,' he had said. But she had been in no mind to be lectured and he hadn't hung around—perhaps thinking that the best way to calm her fears was for him to absent himself.

Mallon spent that Monday in making tea for the builders and in feeling thoroughly mortified at the way she had behaved with Harris yesterday. She knew she was not going to feel any better until she had apologised.

Strangely, bearing in mind she had an uncomfortable weight on her conscience, that night she had her first dream-free sleep in a long while. She awoke on Tuesday to another sunny morning and went to one of her windows to look out at the peace and serenity of it all—before the builders came—and could not help but realise that Harcourt House had been built in a most wonderful spot.

With the improvement in the weather, so Mallon's 'sunnier' side began to reassert itself. So much so that when she saw that one of the builders had left a newspaper lying around, she borrowed it. The only live-in job that remotely appealed—and in all honesty it wasn't all that appealing—was a hotel receptionist's job. She now thought she would be able to do that sort of work but, did she want to?

The knowledge that in less than three months she would have to find somewhere to live and work, if she didn't want to go and park herself on her mother and John, prodded her into putting pen to paper. But it was Thursday before Mallon, impatient with herself for her delaying tactics, firmly decided to go and post her application.

She was uncertain how near or far was the closest postbox, and went to see if Kevin and the van were anywhere about. He was usually gone, or going, somewhere. The van was not to be seen. 'Kev won't be back for a couple of hours,' Dean informed her helpfully. 'If it's urgent, though, you can borrow my bike,' he offered.

Mallon knew that Dean was a cycling enthusiast. 'Are you sure?' she asked.

'It's not my best bike,' he answered with a shy smile.

And five minutes later, able to prove the old adage 'You never forget how to ride a bike' Mallon was having a lovely time pedalling up the road. She did not see a postbox until she was almost at Sherwins' shop. But, having popped her letter inside the postbox, she was enjoying herself so much that on her way back she investigated the various lanes *en route*. By the time Harcourt House came into view, Mallon had a feeling she would be very reluctant to leave the area.

Having departed with more determination not to wobble off the bike than with style,

Mallon pedalled back up the drive with both style and speed—but only to have to concentrate on not falling off in her surprise when, at one and the same time, she spotted Harris and his large car.

She sailed straight past him and went to return Dean's bike. 'Thank you, Dean,' she said with a smile.

'You can borrow it any time,' he replied, which she thought was lovely of him, and she thanked him again, but owned to feeling all kind of churned up inside; and knew it had nothing to do with the fact that this was the first time she had ridden a bike in years.

She was approaching the rear entrance when Harris came round the corner and joined her. 'Whose chariot?' he enquired by way of greeting.

'Dean's,' she answered. And, realising that that probably didn't mean very much to him. 'Charlie's mate,' she added, 'the plumber.' They entered the house and, when she just knew Harris wasn't asking for an explanation found she was burbling on, 'I borrowed it to go and post off a job application.'

Harris halted. She halted with him. 'You're not happy here?' he asked.

Mallon stared at him, then glanced pointedly around at the clutter of builders' essentials lying around in the hall. Added to that was the general banging and clattering going on, and she didn't have to say a word—they both laughed.

To share laughter with him did funny things to her insides. 'I'm just about to make some coffee,' she invented. 'Would you like one?'

'I thought I'd have to make my own,' he accepted, and smiled at her, and she went hastily in front of him to the kitchen.

'You're not working today?' she asked when they were seated at the kitchen table, their coffee in front of them, a sudden feeling of being on edge starting to get to her. 'Sorry, that was stupid, you obviously are.' Would he wear a business suit purely to come and have a look at a building site, for goodness' sake?

'You're nervous of me?' he asked, too shrewd by half in her view. But, when only a short while ago his quick perception might have bothered her, strangely, just then, it didn't.

'Not nervous,' she answered, and, as if to prove it, sent him a smile. 'What I am feeling is awkward and guilty because I know I owe you one big apology, and I don't know the best way to go about it.'

Grey eyes fixed on her lovely deep blue ones. 'Such honesty,' he said quietly, adding, 'I appreciate it, Mallon. But don't feel awkward—I take it, since there's not much here worth breaking, that the apology you owe me is personal?'

'You know it is. You came here last weekend to unwind, but my—jumpy—behaviour last Sunday drove you back to London earlier than you intended.'

'You've been feeling guilty about that?' he questioned seriously.

She nodded. 'And ashamed,' she confessed.

'Oh, Mallon, Mallon,' he said softly. 'You've been through such a foul time. It's only natural that you're going to be jumpy on occasion.' He left his chair and, coming over to where she was sitting, he looked down at her and, smiling, tapped her gently on her nose, and stated, 'And I shouldn't have let it get to me that you can't trust me enough to believe me when I tell you that you're safe with me.'

'Oh, Harris, I...' she began helplessly, realising only then that he was far more sensitive than she had seen. But he had moved a few steps away and was transferring his coffee cup and saucer from the table to the draining board.

'Don't worry about it,' he instructed, and, going on to another subject entirely, 'I thought I'd take some time out this morning to come and have a look around and check a few things out with Bob Miller. I could take you for a quick lunch in town afterwards if you're interested?'

She did like him so. A quick lunch didn't sound so good for his digestion, but it pleased her that he had asked. 'Or I could fix you something here?' she offered.

'Thank you, I accept,' he said without hesitation, and she smiled and he went to inspect the rebuilding progress so far.

By the sound of it he wanted to start back for London as soon as he'd eaten. Which she translated as meaning that he wouldn't mind having his meal more or less straight away. Pasta seemed the order of the day.

Harris was back a half-hour later. 'Ready to eat?' Mallon asked.

'I'm impressed,' he commented, and was appreciative too when they sat down to eat.

'You'd no idea you'd be feeding me this lunchtime, but this is excellent.'

'Oh, just something I threw together,' she laughed, thankful she'd found a tin of salmon in a cupboard which, with the pasta, some milk and Roquefort cheese, made a tasty impromptu meal.

She owned she was feeling happy. Though, nearing the end of the meal, when Harris explained that he'd come down today because he would not be there at the weekend, she experienced the oddest sensation which, had she not known better, she would have said was one of disappointment.

Which was quite, quite, utterly ridiculous, she determined. Especially since as soon as he came in she would have been off to a hotel, and would see nothing of him at the weekend anyhow. And why, for heaven's sake, would she want to see him? Crazy wasn't the word for it.

Putting such thoughts aside, Mallon strove to remember what they had been talking about. His property, this property, and his visit today to inspect it, that was it. 'What made you choose this particular area?' she asked. 'Was it because your sister...?' Her voice tailed off.

But Harris, it seemed, was right on her wave-length.

'Faye wasn't living in Lower Macey then,' he took up, bringing out into the open what Mallon was reluctant to. 'She spotted Almora Lodge on her first visit here. When she discovered the owners were renting it out while they're abroad for a year, she persuaded Phillips to take it.' Harris paused, and then quietly asked, 'You've seen nothing of him, I hope?'

'No, thank goodness,' she answered abruptly, bleakly, and guessed her expression must have given away that she regretted having instigated this conversation and did not want to be reminded of his brother-in-law.

But, even so, Haris wasn't prepared to leave the subject, and asked, 'How about those bad dreams?', clearly associating her night-time horrors with Roland Phillips's assault on her.

Mallon made a determined effort to buck up. 'They've gone,' she answered cheerfully.

'Completely?'

'Haven't had one since...' She had been about to say Sunday night, but, feeling sensitive to Harris suddenly, did not want to remind him of their spat last Sunday, so changed it to, 'For three nights.'

She could tell he had immediately done the calculation and that his arithmetic was spot on, but all he said was, 'Keep up the good work.' And then he asked, 'Do you want a hand with the washing up?', although he was plainly about to leave.

And Mallon wanted to laugh and actually did feel light-hearted. 'I think I'll be able to manage,' she replied sunnily—and he left.

She missed him when he had gone, and wondered if she had gone soft in the head. Why, she barely knew the man! What the Dickens was she thinking of?

What she was thinking of, she discovered on Saturday morning, was Harris. He seemed always to be popping into her head. Well, why wouldn't he? she argued. If it hadn't been for him that day she had run from Roland Phillips, heaven alone knew what she would have done.

The builders were working that morning, and it was a lovely day. There was much noise going on, more than usual, or so it seemed, and Mallon thought it a good idea to take a walk. She took her purse with her. If she saw a telephone kiosk she would ring her mother.

Out on the country road, she walked along, her mind absently engaged in wondering what Harris was doing this weekend. Did the fact that he wasn't coming down to Harcourt House mean that he was heavily engaged with some woman? Mallon—ridiculously, she owned—felt a touch irked at the very idea— then became aware of a car approaching from behind.

There was no pavement. She stepped from the road and onto the grass verge. But instead of the car passing, as she'd expected, it started to slow down. She was about to turn to see if some stranger to the area wanted to ask directions, when she heard a voice that turned her blood to ice!

'Can I give you a lift?'

It was Roland Phillips's voice! She was sure of it! She wanted to run, and did not answer. Then the car was pulling in front—and he had recognised her.

'Well, well! As I live and breathe, Mallon Braithwaite!' She kept on walking. He drove alongside of her. 'Now what, I wonder, are you doing in these parts?' She tried to ignore him, but found that his evil brain was clearly up to checking that the only property along that route was the one owned by his brother-in-law. 'Don't tell me you're staying at Harcourt House!'

She wouldn't dream of telling him anything, but dread entered her heart; she didn't want this man knowing where she lived, or that this weekend she would be there on her own.

'You're living with Harris Quillian?' he chortled. 'Now isn't that a turn-up for the books.'

'I'm his caretaker!' Mallon stopped to reply, anger taking the place of fear.

'That's a new name for it!' Mallon realised that Roland Phillips was a man who *would* think like that, and wished that Harris had hit him harder. 'Is he down this weekend?' Roland Phillips asked, to strike fear into her heart again.

'I'll give him your regards when I get back, shall I?' she managed to stay composed long enough to enquire, looking pointedly at Roland Phillips's chin in the hope that the memory of Harris thumping him hadn't disappeared in a bleary haze.

She gathered that it hadn't when he gave her a spiteful look, and put his foot to the accelerator and drove on. She had been enjoying her walk, but all her pleasure had abruptly departed. She turned about and returned to the house.

The builders departed just after midday and, left on her own, Mallon wished she had asked them to take her into town. Any one of them would have done so, she was fairly sure. It wouldn't have taken her long to find some place to stay.

Against that, though, and for all it was sunny now, the weather had been extremely changeable of late, and it did not follow that it was going to stay sunny. As she had told Roland Phillips, she was there at Harcourt House in the capacity of caretaker. Which meant she needed to be on site, at least in case fresh leaks appeared.

Mallon went up to bed that night feeling full of anxiety and praying that her ex-employer had remembered, and believed her, when she had intimated that Harris was around that weekend.

She made doubly sure that her bedroom door was locked and did something she hadn't had to do since she and her mother had parted company with the Jenkins pair—Mallon placed a solid chair under the door handle.

Before she climbed into bed, while perfectly aware that she couldn't see Roland Phillips, drunk or sober, shinning up a drainpipe, she checked that her bedroom windows were locked.

That night her dark dreams returned, and left her so shaken that she couldn't even leave her room to go down to her usual haven of the kitchen.

She was never more glad to see Monday arrive and, with it, the return of the builders. She went with Kevin into town and did some shopping, and tried a couple of times to phone her mother, but she was out, probably shopping herself, Mallon realised.

As the week went on, so Mallon slowly began to get back to the way she had been before she had taken that walk last Saturday. As yet, however, she hadn't been able to say goodbye to the returned dreams and flashbacks.

There was a letter for her on Friday. The receptionist's job she had applied for had been filled. Mallon admitted that she was not overly upset—her dormant sunny temperament seemed to be waking up again. Even the fact that the weather had turned dull, and that Charlie had turned the water off when she had some laundry in the washing machine didn't bother her unduly.

'Got a bit of a problem,' Charlie explained, and explained in detail while she tried to keep up with his plumbing talk.

Anticipating that Harris would arrive at some time on Saturday morning, Mallon cadged a lift with Kevin when he popped in to say he was going to Sherwins and did she want anything. She returned with fresh vegetables and chicken pieces, with the idea of making a large casserole. She would have some for her dinner that evening—then, if Harris didn't want to go out or start foraging for his meal tomorrow, he could have the rest of it. If he didn't, it would keep in the fridge for her meal when she returned on Sunday.

The last of the builders had gone by five-thirty. At six o'clock the casserole was in the oven and was coming along nicely, when she heard the sound of a car pulling up. One of the builders returning for something he had forgotten? Or—she felt a glow of anticipation suddenly—had Harris come down today instead of tomorrow?

Unsure if her feeling of warmth was in evidence in her eyes and face, Mallon turned her back on the windows. Harris usually passed the windows in his car, but that wasn't to say that some builders' plant wasn't blocking the way. If it was Harris and he was walking by, he might glance in.

She had herself under control when she heard someone coming along the hall. If it was one of the builders he could have taken what he'd come back for and gone. If it was something he had left inside, she was sure that whichever one of them it was would have called out.

The kitchen door opened, but as she turned and glanced to the door, so the colour drained from her face. 'This place is taking shape!' Roland Phillips remarked, coming further into the kitchen.

Mallon felt sick in the pit of her stomach. 'What do you want?' she asked bluntly.

'Don't be like that, Mallon. I've come to do you a favour.'

'I don't need your favours!'

'Yes, you do. Your mother rang.'

'My m...'

'Shame on you, Mallon.' He tut-tutted. 'Couldn't you bring yourself to tell her you'd left me in the lurch?'

'I thought it best not to tell her why I left!' Mallon retorted. Oh, heaven help her, she was here all alone, not a builder in sight—and Roland Phillips had got that lecherous look in his eyes! 'She would have insisted I went to the police.' Mallon thought it would do no harm to warn him.

'Don't be like that, my dear,' he replied, his eyes going over her figure. 'You know I've always fancied you.'

'You don't know me!' she answered shortly, backing away as he came closer.

'Whose fault is that?' he complained, and as he took another step nearer, and she smelt his alcoholic breath, Mallon had nowhere else to go. 'Why can't we...?' he began, but the rest of it was lost in the roar of sound from the doorway.

'What the hell are you doing here?' Harris Quillian demanded, his face like thunder.

Roland Phillips jerked round. 'I—I...' he started to bluster. Then got his second wind and edged away from Mallon, his prey, to challenge, albeit not very aggressively, 'If you'd got a phone here I wouldn't have had to bother to come at all. I came to tell Mallon that her mother had phoned.'

Harris wasn't interested. 'I don't want you anywhere near here,' he told him curtly, holding the kitchen door wide. 'Get out, and stay out!' And, his tone icy and determined, he snarled threateningly, 'Set so much as one foot on this property again…and I shall come looking for you.'

He didn't say what he would do when he found him. He didn't have to. Roland Phillips quite plainly knew that his brother-in-law didn't go around making empty threats, and didn't hang around to say goodbye. He went at speed.

By then Mallon, although she owned to feeling a shade weepy in her relief that Harris had arrived tonight instead of tomorrow, though still shaken was starting to recover. 'I wasn't expecting you until tomorrow!' she exclaimed.

But was shaken anew that it seemed Harris had put his own interpretation on having seen her and his brother-in-law so up close together. 'Obviously!' he rapped.

'Obviously?' she repeated, thunderstruck. 'You can't for a minute think…!'

'How did Phillips know you were here?' Harris Quillian demanded.

And Mallon *did* want to weep. How could he? How *could* he? But her spirit, badly shaken on two counts, was aided by sudden fury. Somehow, she managed to control her fury, and it was with dignity when, not deigning to answer him and passing the oven as she went, 'Turn that off at seven!' she ordered. 'I'm going to pack!'

The pig, the absolute total pig! She sailed from the room, head held high, and stormed up the stairs. She was so incensed she only just remembered to sidestep the dodgy floorboard on the landing that Cyril had pointed out that morning, and arrived in her room growing more and more outraged. So outraged, in fact, that she slammed the door with such force the windows rattled.

She was unrepentant; she didn't care. The place was a disaster area anyway, with its disintegrating floorboards, haphazard plumbing, perished plaster in most bedrooms that left only two habitable. Mallon was too het up as she got out her cases to want to think of its beautiful setting and how gloriously fabulous it was going to look when all the work had been completed.

How dared Harris-rotten-Quillian think that she had *obviously* contacted Roland Phillips to come over as soon as the last workman had gone because Harris-rotten-Quillian would *obviously* not be arriving until the morning?

Hurt and angry, and feeling more like bursting into tears than ever, Mallon had just taken a couple of dresses out from the wardrobe when her bedroom door opened and the object of her hate came in. She knew the chair was in the way—it was a heavy chair and by skirting round she was spared from nightly having to drag it across the room. Harris nearly fell over it.

Good! 'I leave the chair there—usually lodged under the doorknob—to keep out unwanted intruders!' she told him acidly, going over to one of the open suitcases on the bed and starting to fold the first of the dresses into it.

Harris watched her for a moment or two, then said, 'I'm not very good at saying sorry.'

Huh! 'Even when you know you're in the wrong?'

'Do you really prop that chair under your doorknob at night?'

She shrugged, intended to tell him noth-ing—but the words were coming anyway. 'I went for a walk last Saturday. Your brother-in-law was driving by. He stopped, and real-ised where I was living. That chair has been under the doorknob ever since.'

'Oh, Mallon,' Harris mourned helplessly. 'I'm a swine.'

'*Obviously!*' she agreed, and wondered if she was losing it when, having tossed his word back at him, she wanted to laugh.

'I *am* sorry,' he stated softly.

'There—that didn't hurt, did it?'

'If I lend you my mobile phone to ring your mother, will you forgive me?'

Mallon hesitated. 'I—might,' she mumbled.

'Your mother doesn't know you no longer work for Phillips?'

'I rang her—from the Clifton Hotel. I couldn't tell her. She'd worry.' Mallon's anger was draining away. She started to fold the sec-ond of the dresses.

'You don't have to leave!' Harris said sud-denly, and Mallon knew, her anger gone, that she did not want to leave. 'In fact, you don't have to go anywhere this weekend.'

'You're staying here?' She was weakening; she knew she was.

'Until Sunday,' he confirmed. 'Try to trust me, Mallon,' he urged. She rather thought that she did trust him already. She looked across to him, looked straight into a pair of steady grey eyes. Then, as they stared at each other, a smile, a winning smile of such charm broke from him that she felt momentarily powerless. 'Please stay,' he urged, and, teasingly, 'I know you're just going to hate me like blazes if, come your return on Sunday, there's none of that delicious-smelling casserole left.'

She wanted to smile in return, but wouldn't. Though owned that, rather than referring to her going and never coming back, he was making it easier for her to return on Sunday—should she still decide to go now.

'Are you saying you won't take me t-to a hotel?' she asked, thereby agreeing, she real-ised, that she was not intending to leave per-manently.

'You know that's not what I'm saying. What I am saying is, given the impossibility of the conditions here, you manage to make the place more and more comfortable each time I visit.

It seems poor recompense that you should leave just because I've arrived.'

He was saying, she saw, that from his point of view she was welcome to stay. But that, should she go, it would be only her choice. To stay, she knew, would be to tell him that trust him she did.

'You no longer think I purposely invited your brother-in-law here?'

'I never did,' Harris replied promptly.

'Oh?'

'So I got mad. I wanted an excuse to hit him. When he scuttled away without a fight— I just needed someone to release my fury on.'

'And I happened to be the nearest.'

'That doesn't make me a very nice person,' he volunteered.

She wanted to deny that. Thinking of his amazing goodness to her, she wanted to tell him so, but felt shy suddenly. 'That halo I gave you did slip a bit,' she agreed. Then smiled as she told him, 'But nobody's perfect.'

Harris returned her smile, and to be friends with him once more did her heart good. 'You want to exchange those cases for a weekend bag?' he suggested.

Mallon shook her head. 'If it's all the same with you...' she took a deep breath '...I'll stay and share that casserole with you.'

Harris nodded, satisfied, then showed her the particular peculiarities of his mobile, and left her. She dialled her mother's number with no idea how to explain why she did not want her to again try and get her on Roland Phillips's number.

'Hello, Mum, it's me,' she opened.

'Oh, Mallon. What a relief! Mr Phillips said you weren't working for him any longer when I rang. Where on earth are you? I've been worried...'

'Oh, Mum, there's no need. I'm not far away from Lower Macey. Only a few miles up the road from that other job.'

'What happened?'

Mallon, while hating to mislead her parent, replied by saying that she hadn't taken to Roland Phillips all that well, and now had a better job working for his brother-in-law, supervising the builders—she was glad brilliant supervisor Bob Miller couldn't hear her—and also overseeing the delivery of furniture, fixtures and fittings to the property. 'It's only a temporary job,' she explained, 'but I really love it.'

'Well, as long as you're happy. You know that there's always a home here for you.'

'Of course. How's John?'

As the phone call was ending, Mallon's mother pressed her to give her new employer's name and, since there was no phone there, the address where Mallon could be contacted. Her mother wanted Mallon to have a word with John, as well.

'Did I hear your mother say you were working for Harris Quillian?' John asked, and, when she confirmed that she was, it transpired that John knew of him, for he went on to say, 'Well, we've no need to worry about you there. Harris Quillian is head of Warren and Taber Finance. A straighter man you'd never find.'

After her telephone call, John reiterating that there was a home there for her any time she liked, Mallon washed her face, applied her usual light make-up and brushed her blonde hair. She felt she would like to have changed into a fresh dress, but Harris didn't seem to miss much and she didn't want him to think she had changed on account of him being there. Besides, who dressed up to eat in the kitchen?

Harris wasn't around when Mallon went back down the stairs again. But she knew he wouldn't be very far away. There were still a couple of hours of daylight left. He would be around somewhere, having a look at how the work had progressed since he was last down.

Mallon had the casserole, some potatoes and broccoli all ready to serve when she heard him approaching the kitchen. 'Everything okay?' she enquired when he came in.

'Some parts of the rebuilding are going on faster than others,' he answered, confirming that he'd been having a look around.

'While I think of it, there's a very dicey floorboard on the landing,' Mallon reported, taking the casserole pot over to the table.

'I noticed it.'

It was true, she mused, he did never miss a thing. She supposed he hadn't got to be head of a finance company by missing very much.

'Where did you learn to cook?' he asked midway through the meal. 'I haven't spotted a recipe book anywhere around.'

'I'm not sure you need much of a recipe book for a casserole,' Mallon answered lightly.

'I've always cooked,' she said without thinking.

'Your mother didn't care to?'

Was he probing to know her background? Mallon eyed him carefully. Or was he just being polite? 'My father's death devastated her,' she replied, seeing no harm in answering in. 'My mother lost interest in everything when he died.'

Harris eyed her in that steady way he had. 'Even you, her daughter?' he enquired quietly.

Mallon could feel herself bridling but, because most of the time she quite liked the man, she decided he was just keeping some sort of conversation going between them 'It was because of me she decided to live on without him,' she replied—a shade coolly, it had to be admitted.

'How old were you when your father died?'

'Thirteen,' Mallon replied, and, remembering back, 'He was a lovely man, quiet, gentle—a wonderful surgeon, so everyone said.'

'He was a consultant?'

'The best in all fields. It's no wonder my mother...ceased to function for a while.' But Mallon did not want to dwell on those unhappy days, and went on brightly, 'My mother married again recently, I think I mentioned it, and, after some truly dreadful unhappy years, is happy again now. And that's what matters.'

'You're saying that there is now no place for you?' Harris queried shrewdly.

'That's exactly what I'm *not* saying,' Mallon denied. 'Only this evening, when I phoned them—your phone's over there by the way—' she broke off to point to the end of the worktop '—they both said that there was a home there for me with them.' And, before he could say anything to that, 'But naturally I prefer living here,' she added dryly.

'Rotting floorboards and all,' Harris took up, his mouth curving in a hint of a smile, not offended in any way. 'You were living with your mother prior to her remarriage?' he asked.

'We had a small flat.' Mallon again saw no reason not to answer. 'My mother would have been upset had I said I wanted to keep the flat on rather than move in with her and John. But it was true that I was looking for a job change.'

'So you made believe you'd be happier doing a live-in housekeeping job?'

'It wasn't all housekeeping. True, Almora Lodge took some clearing up, but I'm not used to being idle and R-Roland Phillips's study was a mess too. He suggested I should sort things out for him, get his backlog of filing filed, that sort of thing. He...' Abruptly, she stopped. She didn't want to think about Roland Phillips, much less talk about him. 'Del brought me some more plums from his trees yesterday. I made a fresh pie, or there's cheese for afters?'

Harris eyed her silently for some seconds, then quietly stated, 'Do you know, Mallon, I rather think I got the better part of the bargain when I asked you to stay on here.'

His remark pleased her, pleased her so much she didn't know what to say. She wanted something sharp and witty but there was nothing there, only a tremendous feeling of shyness. She swallowed hard, and then managed, 'And you think that sort of remark gets you out of the washing up?'

'There's a dishwasher here somewhere,' he murmured, good humour there in his fine grey eyes.

Mallon declared that they hadn't used sufficient dishes to warrant the dishwasher, and later Harris did the drying while she washed and rinsed—and again that feeling of shyness crept over her. It seemed so intimate somehow, standing so close next to him. She moved her position, taking half a step away. Good heavens, what in creation was going on with her? Intimate! For goodness' sake, what was she thinking? Harris was merely helping with the washing up—he'd be astounded if he knew what had just gone through her head.

She turned from him, checking that everything was neat and tidy. 'I think I'll go to bed!' she announced shortly, suddenly feeling more aware of Harris than she had of any man, and that, most peculiarly, included Keith Morgan.

She looked up at Harris, and found he had his eyes on her, that steady look of his fixed on her again. 'You usually go to bed this early?' he asked. It was still daylight outside.

'N-not usually. But you're here to caretake tonight, so I feel free to go up and finish my book.'

'You could bring your book down to the drawing room,' he suggested mildly.

'I'll—um—see,' she mumbled, but left the kitchen knowing that she wouldn't be coming down from her room with her book—she had an uncomfortable feeling that he knew it too.

It wasn't as if she didn't trust him, she reasoned, when up in her room she tried to make sense of her emotions. It had to be emotional, this feeling of being at one with him one minute, and shy and a touch diffident with him the next.

She did trust him; she knew that she did. So much so that, knowing that there were just the two of them alone in the house, that night she restored the heavy chair by the door to its former home. She realised a couple of hours later, when she lay down to go to sleep, that her trust in Harris must have been instinctive and complete, because she had not locked her door and, remembering that it was unlocked, she couldn't think of one good reason to get out of bed to go and lock it.

Having gone to sleep in a fairly tranquil frame of mind, her dreams that night, in contrast, seemed doubly violent. Mallon was gasping and panicking in her sleep. She seemed to know that she was dreaming, that it wasn't real, but as panic held her firmly down she could not find a way through to the surface. Dark forces were squashing her; she was drowning. Her breathing stopped, there was no more air; she could take none in. Then, just when she knew she must suffocate, she broke through—and surfaced.

With a gasp of terror, Mallon came awake, fighting for breath. She inhaled on a noisy gulp of air and struggled to sit up, and gradually her laboured breathing started to ease. She was all right; she was all right. It was a dream, only a dream—but she didn't want to go back to sleep again, didn't want it to start all over again.

In fear she got out of bed and went to the window, intending to open it wide. She needed air, cool cold air. Then her brain started to function again. Harris was next door. The sound of a window opening might disturb his sleep.

Mallon turned away, knowing she should go back to bed, but she couldn't; her fears of it all starting up again were too real. She grabbed up her cotton robe, glad then that she had taken the chair away from the door and had no need to start moving furniture about.

It was still dark when she quietly opened her door, but she didn't want to put the light on in case Harris heard any small sound or perhaps opened his eyes and saw a line of light. Just in time she remembered the ropy floorboard, and, avoiding it, found her way to the banister and held on to it as a guide all the way down the stairs.

Having safely negotiated her way to the bottom, Mallon knew of the perils in the way of builders' materials lying about, but felt she could safely put a light on now.

She was by then wide awake and did not want to return to her room, to fall asleep again and to again awake in panic. She went quietly along the hall to the outside door. Harris had locked up tonight.

Mallon unlocked the door and went and stood outside in the cold night air, breathing deeply until after about five minutes she began to feel calmer. Calm enough to return indoors anyway.

Taking care to be quiet, she stepped back inside and re-locked the outside door. She knew that she still didn't want to return to her bed, and, as she had on several occasions before in the middle of the night, she headed for the kitchen. Strangely, though, she saw that the kitchen door was ajar and that the light was on.

She realised that Harris must have forgotten to turn off the light before he'd gone to bed—though she couldn't remember noticing the light was on. Mallon put that down to the fact that she had been in something of a state earlier.

But, on pushing the door open, she was staggered to see Harris standing at the kitchen sink calmly filling the kettle with water. 'I disturbed you!' she exclaimed at once.

'Can't a man make a cup of tea in his own kitchen without you kicking up a fuss?' he enquired pleasantly.

She felt dreadful. The poor man had come down to Harcourt House for a rest, to unwind, and here he was up in the middle of the night, and it was all her fault. 'I'm sorry,' she apologised, feeling utterly miserable, and turned about to go back up to her suddenly much detested bed. But his voice delayed her.

'Bad dream?' he asked, and she turned back.

'I—thought I'd said goodbye to them, but they returned,' she admitted.

'When?' he enquired, spooning tea into the teapot. 'When did they come back?'

'Last Saturday night.' She did not seem to have the energy just then to prevaricate.

'The Saturday you were out walking and met Phillips again,' Harris remarked, not having to pause to calculate, she realised. But he made no further comment on that subject, but invited, 'Come and sit down and share a pot of tea with me. Unless you'd prefer something stronger.'

'Tea would be fine,' Mallon answered. But barely had she agreed to stay and drink tea with him than she suddenly became aware that, where she was nightdress and cotton-robe-clad, Harris wore only a robe. From his nicely shaped legs showing beneath and the vee of dark hair at his chest, it would seem that he had little else underneath. Abruptly she went and took a seat at the kitchen table.

'Sugar?'

'What?'

'Do you take sugar?' Harris enquired.

'Er—no,' she replied, and made stern efforts to get herself more of one piece. 'I didn't think I'd made any noise. I didn't want to disturb you.'

'You didn't. I was awake, wondering if I started moving around I might wake you—when I heard a few isolated sounds that indicated you might be in trouble.'

'Oh, Harris, I'm a mess, aren't I?'

He looked at her, and then brought two cups of tea over. 'No, you're not,' he answered, pulling out a chair and sitting down opposite her. 'What you are is traumatised by what happened to you, or would have happened to you had you not been able to escape from Phillips.'

Mallon stared at him. Harris seemed so understanding somehow. She felt then that she could talk to him about absolutely anything. 'But—I should be over that by now, surely?'

'Not at all,' he disagreed, sending her a gentle smile. 'You're highly sensitive, Mallon. You went to live and work at Almora Lodge in good faith—your faith that Phillips was a decent man was cruelly shattered.' Harris broke off, and then, his grey eyes holding her deeply blue ones, refusing to let her look away, said deliberately, 'It hasn't been of any help that something similar happened to you before.'

'No, it didn't!' she denied sharply, her calmer mood swiftly vanishing.

Annoyingly, Harris stayed quiet, his eyes still holding hers, still refusing to allow her to look away. 'Forgive me,' he said, but didn't look particularly sorry. 'You said, that day we met, that you'd had your fill of men who seemed to think you couldn't wait to get into bed with them.'

'Do you forget nothing either?' Mallon erupted.

'Either?' he queried.

'I've already seen that you don't appear to miss much!' she retorted. He had rattled her; she didn't see why she shouldn't try to rattle him.

But, no, he stayed calm, stayed cool, and not one whit out of countenance. 'I haven't missed that, while there's a warmth in you that wants to get out, you are very often—troubled—in case that warmth is taken advantage of.'

He was psychoanalysing again; she didn't like it. 'What sort of night-time reading do you have by the side of your bed?' she asked sarcastically.

He smiled, it was a lovely smile, and something inside her seemed to melt. And when, gently, he asked, 'What happened, Mallon, to make you so defensive?' while she wanted to hotly deny she was in any way defensive, she found that she could not.

'N...' She tried anyway, but the word 'nothing' refused to leave her lips. 'I...' she tried again. Then found she was relating, rather shakily, it had to be admitted, 'Two years after my father's death my mother married again. It was a disaster from almost the first.'

'What went wrong?' Harris prompted, his tone quiet.

'He, Ambrose Jenkins, was more interested in my father's money than in making my mother happy,' Mallon replied, and looked away from Harris as she relived that dreadful time. 'By the time the marriage was over, there was no money left. Even the lovely house my father had bought was gone.'

'You and your mother moved into your small flat without this man?'

Mallon nodded. 'And without his odious son!' she declared.

'But his son lived with you in your previous home?'

'That's where I learned the value of propping a chair under my bedroom doorknob if I wanted any privacy.'

'He tried to seduce you?' Harris questioned gently.

'It didn't get beyond him trying to make a grab for me when no one else was around.'

'How old were you?'

'When it began? Fifteen. Though it didn't start with his father until I was sixteen.'

'His father! G...' Harris bit off whatever expletive had been on his tongue.

'He was more verbal than grabbing.'

'What was your mother doing all this time?' Harris wanted to know.

'Doing?' Mallon flicked a glance at him. 'Nothing. She didn't know. Besides, I made jolly certain I was never alone in the same room with either of them.'

'Good for you. But—you didn't tell your mother what you were having to put up with?'

'How could I? She had barely been functioning after my father's death. She later on realised her new husband was a lecher, but to know then that she had married such a man, brought him into our home, and that he and his equally lecherous son were both casting their lascivious gaze in my direction, would have finished her.'

'And so you bore it all alone?'

'It's over now,' Mallon said, and actually found a smile.

'But it's left its scars.'

'I'll cope,' she said lightly.

'I'm sure you will,' he agreed.

And she liked him so well then, as she looked into his warm grey eyes, she actually felt quite a lump in her throat. Abruptly she got to her feet. 'Do you mind if I don't drink my tea after all?' she asked, conversely then feeling somehow that she needed the sanctuary of her own room.

Harris got to his feet too, his tea untouched also. 'What's wrong?' he wanted to know.

'Nothing,' she answered. Then, staring up into his good-looking face, she confessed, 'I've shared, told you things just now, that I've never told another living soul.' She smiled. 'I think I feel a little light-headed.'

'Your confidences are safe with me,' he quietly assured her.

'I know,' she replied, and did.

'Come on, let's get you back to bed. You've got to be up early in the morning.'

She laughed, the sauce of it! He was here—he was good at making tea. Let him make Bob Miller his first brew. Switching off the downstairs lights, and then switching on the stairs and landing lights, Harris went up the staircase with her.

'Watch that floorboard,' he warned when they turned on to the landing.

She recalled how he had noticed it previously but glanced at him to remind him that *she* had been the one to tell him about that floorboard! But, not looking where she was going, her foot unerringly found that rickety floorboard. It gave way and she started to fall knowing, as she grabbed at air, that nothing was going to save her.

Something did, though. Or rather, Harris reached for her to try and hold her, but in his efforts he wasn't looking where he was walking either, and he caught his foot in the same floorboard—and they both went down.

Mallon was about to laugh, to apologise, to say something light—perhaps something about his hazard-strewn house. But then she became startlingly aware of his body moving over the top of her, his weight pressing down on her through the thin covering of her nightdress and cotton robe—and she wasn't stopping to think that his weight might be just temporary while he recovered and attempted to find his feet.

'Get off me!' she shrieked, her hands pushing at his chest.

'Shh-shh,' he quieted her, and as she looked up at him and saw nothing of the lust in his face that she had seen in the faces of Ambrose and Lee Jenkins, or Roland Phillips, so her world started to right itself. 'Never in a million years, remember?' Harris murmured.

And she felt ashamed of herself. 'Sorry,' she mumbled. But suddenly the feel of his body over hers was creating the oddest of sensations in her. 'I—do trust you,' she managed. 'It's j-just that…'

'Old habits die hard.'

'Something like that,' Mallon replied, and as Harris made to get up, so she stared up at him. He hesitated, his eyes on her eyes, his glance going down to her mouth, and back up again to her eyes.

Then, unhurriedly, his head was coming down, and tenderly he placed his mouth over hers. Mallon felt the warmth of his kiss, and was not conscious of breathing. All she knew was that this gentle kiss from his wonderful mouth was totally thrilling. She wanted to kiss him back, but was afraid to move lest she break some spell. So she just lay there, closer to him than she had ever been to any man, and too soon Harris was breaking his kiss.

He looked down at her. 'There's nothing to worry about, Mallon,' he assured her, his tones soothing. 'I—um—think you needed to be kissed, and—' he smiled '—while it wasn't such a great chore—did anyone ever tell you what an invitingly sensational mouth you have?—that kiss was a prelude to nothing.'

Her heart was thundering like crazy. 'I—er...' Her voice was husky, but she wasn't surprised. 'If you'll let me up?' she requested, and searched desperately for some suitably light remark. And, as he got to his feet and helped her up, 'Let me know when you think *you* need to be kissed,' she said, 'and I'll see what I can do about it.' It wasn't brilliant or witty, but it was the best she could do in the circumstances.

She went to her room without another word, and, closing the door, leant against it, her head in a whirl. She had been kissed with more passion, but never so wonderfully. Harris had said that his kiss had been a prelude to nothing. But—she hadn't wanted that kiss to lead to nothing! She had wanted him to kiss her again, and again! Heavens above, what on earth was happening to her?

CHAPTER FIVE

By MORNING Mallon had her head back together again. While she was still slightly amazed at the emotional feelings Harris had aroused in her when he had kissed her so tenderly, so wonderfully, last night, she was able to convince herself that, clad as they had been, in the situation they'd been in when they had fallen in a heap together, something of the sort was not unlikely to happen.

She would watch out in future, of course. Not that the same thing would happen again. She was never ever going to leave her room in the middle of the night. Nothing, not even the vilest screaming nightmare, would make her.

She owned she was feeling just a touch out of sorts that morning. A fact not helped by the event that her shower had gone temperamental on her—she'd have a word with the plumber if he were about. Harris had said she had 'needed' to be kissed. So, okay, he had also said that it wasn't such a great chore, but his

146

remark wasn't very complimentary, was it? Now she came to think of it, it was a down-right cheek! She would prefer to be kissed because he just couldn't help it, rather than from some 'there-there, that'll make you feel better'-type diagnosis.

She there and then decided to avoid him as much as possible. It was too late now to wish she had gone to a hotel last night. And it would draw too much attention to her feeling out of sorts if she suggested she should stay at a hotel tonight.

Having washed and dressed, Mallon went downstairs to find that Harris must already be up and about—the cups and saucers they had left on the kitchen table last night had been washed and put away at any rate.

She glanced through the kitchen window and saw him in conversation with Bob Miller. Bob was earlier than usual—had it been pre-arranged he should be early, or had Harris phoned him that morning?

Mallon was not left wondering for long. She had just made a pot of tea when Harris came into the kitchen, his glance going over her long-legged trim shape in her jeans and tee shirt.

'How's my favourite caretaker?' he asked easily, coming over and looking down into her face as if to assess for himself how she was.

'Never better,' she answered lightly—no way was he going to know that he bothered her in the slightest. 'Baz brought me some new laid eggs from his hens yesterday. Boiled or scrambled?' She met his glance, but just had to look at his truly wonderful mouth, and felt her heart give a little leap when she saw his lips start to curve upwards. She looked swiftly away.

'I haven't had a newly-laid boiled egg in years,' he replied.

Mallon poured some tea and handed Bob Miller his through the kitchen window, and, feeling unsettled and jumpy inside, she got busy setting the eggs to boil.

'Have you heard from the job you wrote after?' Harris enquired conversationally when they were seated at the table.

'Are you asking me to leave?' she asked jerkily, and knew she was more jumpy—about him—than she had realised. Especially when he looked at her in some surprise.

'What brought that on?' he asked, and, when she went a touch pink with embarrassment, 'Haven't I just said that you're my favourite caretaker?'

'So...' She shrugged. 'I heard—they didn't want me.'

'Their loss is my gain,' he replied, and she just didn't need his charm. 'Talking of leaving, though,' he went on, 'it might be an idea if you made yourself scarce today.'

Solemnly she looked at him. 'But you're not asking me to leave?'

'Definitely not,' he replied, and informed her, 'There is more than one rotting floorboard on the landing. I've arranged for all the old wood to be taken up and a new floor put down today. It's only a guess, but I'd say the noise is going to be fairly horrendous.'

Mallon was used to the builders' racket, but she saw his point. 'Thanks for the tip-off.'

'I could drive you into town—you could shop to your heart's content,' he offered.

But there was a restlessness in her which Mallon couldn't understand, and all she knew was that to sit beside him in the close confines of his car was not part of her avoid-him-as-much-as-possible plan.

'It's a lovely day. I think I'll go for a walk—a long walk,' she answered, and immediately recalled how last Saturday she had been taking a walk when she had seen Roland Phillips again.

Grey eyes assessed deeply blue eyes. 'Would you like company?' Harris asked carefully, and, because she was feeling all at once extremely sensitively tuned in to his wavelength, it seemed to Mallon that Harris was remembering Roland Phillips too.

She answered slowly, but truthfully, 'I think there are some things I should do on my own.'

Harris smiled encouragingly. 'That's my—er—caretaker,' he said. But she felt a warm glow and inordinately pleased.

She set off as soon as the breakfast things had been cleared away, and walked steadily along green leafy lanes. She wasn't making for anywhere in particular, but she had some money with her should she come across a shop.

As she had remarked to Harris, it was a lovely day, and, having endured enough rain, it was a pleasure to be out in the sun. He had offered to walk with her and she had declined, but he was in her head so much on that walk it was just as though he was there walking along beside her.

Mallon had no idea how far she had walked until all at once she recognised that she was in the area of Sherwins' shop. It seemed as good a stopping place as any.

Though as she rounded the bend to the shop, so she recognised someone coming out from Sherwins and going over to his parked car. Roland Phillips. What she could have done, because he hadn't yet seen her, was to have doubled back and disappeared down the side lane she had just come from, and stayed there until he had gone by.

She did hesitate, it was true, but suddenly she was remembering Harris saying 'That's my caretaker' and she knew that to run away was no way to slay her personal dragons.

She went on; he saw her and he stopped. 'Well, if it isn't my brother-in-law's little play-mate,' he remarked nastily, his eyes doing a thorough inspection of her nevertheless. Mallon went to walk past him without a word—he didn't seem to like it. Though, ever with his eye to the main chance, 'I'm going your way. I'll give you a lift if you like?'

'No, thank you.'

'Come on—don't be stuck up,' he said, and tried to delay her by placing a hand on her arm.

Mallon found his touch revolting but, instead of being afraid, she suddenly discovered she was growing angry. 'Take your hand off me!' she ordered cuttingly.

'Don't be like that!' he answered with what he thought was a winning smile—and Mallon was all at once as angry with herself as she was with him. To think she had let this excuse for a man, this oily weasel, cause her such ghastly nights!

'I do not like you,' she started to grow furious enough to tell him. 'In fact I find you totally repulsive.' And, her indignation never higher, 'Normally I wouldn't lower myself to speak to the likes of you,' she told him scornfully. 'But I'll make an exception this once to tell you that if you ever come near me again, I shall not hesitate to report your attack on me to the police.'

He didn't like it. She didn't care, and, since she had nothing else she wanted to say to him, she pulled her arm from his slackening hold and went to take a browse round Sherwins.

From Sherwins she started to make her way back to Harcourt House. Had she thought about it she would have assumed she would have felt like bursting into tears after her encounter with Roland Phillips—but she felt more elated than anything else.

It was so good not to feel afraid any longer, and while it was true that physically that disgusting man could get the better of her, he was an intelligent man. Intelligent enough anyhow to know that any sniff that he had assaulted a woman and his executive job with a very well-thought-of company would be decidedly rocky, to say the least. She wondered why she hadn't reasoned that out before, and could only suppose that fear of the man had numbed her brain.

The nearer she got to Harcourt House, however, and thoughts of Roland Phillips began to fade. Thoughts of Harris began to dominate her head, instead. She wondered what he was doing while the carpenters were busy putting down a new timber landing. And unexpectedly felt quite churned up that, having come down to Harcourt House to relax, he might have been driven out by the noise and returned to London.

Her eyes scanned the drive for his car as she passed between the stone pillars of his Upper Macey residence. Most of the builders had finished for the day, but Bob Miller's vehicle was there out front, so too was Cyril's car and two others, but neither of them belonged to Harris.

She told herself she wasn't worried. Good heavens, why should she worry? Harris had every right to come and go as he pleased. But when, with the front door open, she could have gone indoors that way, she opted to go round to the rear of the house. His car wasn't there either.

Mallon went into the kitchen, her earlier feeling of elation completely gone. If anything she was feeling a shade flat. Though, of course, she knew that was only because, extra carpenters brought in, the noise was occasionally deafening.

At half past four the floor was down and the building workers went on their way. Since they wouldn't be back until Monday, Mallon got out the broom and, after sweeping the landing, she swept the stairs and the downstairs hall. Some of the dust and debris went out of the rear door, but the dust and debris that was nearer to the front door she swept out that way.

She was in the act of sweeping off the front steps when an electrical wholesaler's van drove in through the gates. She stood watching, hoping that the driver hadn't seen her from the road and called in to ask for directions to somewhere—apart from Sherwins and Almora Lodge, she was a stranger in these parts herself.

'Miss Braithwaite?' the driver got out to enquire, and before she could answer, 'Got your TV for you,' he said.

She opened her mouth, but started to smile—Harris's car was coming up the drive. She turned her attention back to the TV man. 'Er—you'd better bring it into the kitchen. I don't think we've got the necessary point in the drawing room.'

'You have,' he assured her. 'One of our chaps came out earlier today.'

'The drawing room it is, then.' She showed him where to take the television set, and was in the kitchen when Harris, having stopped to have a word with the man, followed her into the kitchen.

He came nearer. 'How was your walk?' he asked evenly, his eyes searching her face as if for anything untoward.

She smiled. She felt good, and didn't want to talk about Roland Phillips. 'Fine,' she answered, and, because Harris seemed to be expecting more of a comment than that, 'I thought you'd gone back to London.'

'Oh, dear, does that mean you're glad or sorry?'

As if she'd tell him! 'That's some television set.' He turned away, but as he strolled out of the kitchen, she was sure he had a smile on his face. She guessed he had gone upstairs to inspect the new landing floor.

She thought she might go up too, and change out of the clothes she had worn all day, but suddenly she felt shy, and while she knew she was being totally ridiculous, she just couldn't get past that barrier of shyness. It was there on the landing that they had last night fallen together and he had kissed her and...

Mallon blanked off such thoughts. For goodness' sake, it had been a kiss, and, while it hadn't been the sort of kiss one gave a maiden aunt, it hadn't been very sexual either.

She concentrated her mind on dinner. She had purchased some minced beef in Sherwins—she hoped Harris liked spaghetti bolognese. When she heard him come down the stairs and go in the direction of the drawing room, Mallon slipped out of the kitchen and up to her room to change. She would dearly have loved to take a shower, but had forgotten to have a word with the plumber.

Washed and changed into a cotton dress, Mallon went downstairs again and found the television installer had gone and that Harris was coming into the kitchen with a couple of boxes of what looked like groceries.

'What have you got there?'

'Probably all the wrong things, but since you wouldn't come with me, what's a mere male to do when he investigates and, I admit, gets carried away, in a supermarket?'

She had to laugh, and was still smiling when she saw that his glance had gone to her mouth. How dear he was. *Dear!* Suddenly astonished by the way her thoughts were going, Mallon's smile abruptly departed. She felt awkward all at once.

'Do you like spaghetti bolognese?' she asked shortly, and knew he was staring at her as though trying to figure out what had so suddenly gone wrong. But, when she was certain he would demand to know why she had, on an instant, changed from smiling to stilted, he let it go.

'Spaghetti bolognese is one of my passions,' he replied mildly. And she knew then that it wasn't and that he was lying.

But she didn't feel like laughing, and after some minutes he went from the kitchen, and a minute or so later she heard the muted sound of the television set.

When about an hour and a half later Harris joined her in the kitchen for dinner, Mallon knew that she was feeling more tense than awkward. She had never felt this way before and couldn't understand it. She thought she might have been able to understand it better had she not liked Harris. But she did like him, very much.

When Harris kept up a smooth flow of conversation throughout the meal, she gradually managed to say goodbye to her inner feeling of tension. She was truly interested when he told her of his plans for the house and how, once the house had been restored, he had plans for the outbuildings. Indeed she had started to feel quite relaxed, so relaxed that she was unsure when the conversation had changed and they began generally discussing books they had both read.

But Harris was standing next to her, drying the dishes as she washed them, when that uncomfortable feeling of tension came over her again.

'That's the lot, I think,' she said, taking a look around to see if they had missed anything. And, all chores done, she thought it best to make herself scarce before he noticed she was uptight about something. She felt she knew him well enough by then to know that he would ask why she was uptight. And how could she tell him when she didn't know why herself?

'I think you've earned an evening sitting in front of the television,' Harris teased, turning to her.

She looked at him, and her heart did a crazy little flip, and she knew then that she felt so fidgety, so on edge, that it was completely beyond her to sit silently with him in the drawing room.

'I—um—think I'll go up,' she answered, feeling dreadful that her voice had come out sounding as stilted as she was feeling. 'I've come to a good part in my book,' she lied.

Harris looked back at her, but his tone was mild when, after surveying her for a second or two, 'We needn't have the television on, if you'd prefer to bring your book down,' he suggested.

Oh, grief, this was terrible. What on earth was the matter with her? 'I think I'll have an early night,' she replied, and, thinking to end the conversation, she went to skirt round him, but only to find he had moved and had stepped in front of her.

'Something the matter, Mallon?' he asked quietly, and she felt worse than ever.

'Nothing,' she replied, sincerely hoping he would allow her to leave it there. 'Honestly,' she added, staring up at him, her deeply blue eyes troubled.

'You know you don't have to worry?' he said, and, looking at her sharply, 'Would you like me to leave?'

Her breath caught. No, she did *not* want him to leave. 'No, I wouldn't!' she answered equally sharply.

'You do know I'm not like Phillips?'

'Of course I know!' she exclaimed. 'And I'm not in the slightest worried! I just want… Goodnight,' she said abruptly.

Harris stared at her for perhaps a second longer, then stepped out of her way. Mallon went quickly. Oh, why, oh, why couldn't she be natural with him? What in creation was it about him that made her so restless one minute, so uptight the next?

She reached the privacy of her room, and knew restlessness again when she experienced an incredible urge to go downstairs again to assure Harris that she trusted him completely, and felt not one moment's disquiet with just the two of them alone under the same roof.

That compulsion, that urge, was so strong that only by telling herself that he would think her some kind of nut who had exaggerated out of all proportion his need to know she was not in the slightest worried, stopped her from giving in.

She picked up her book and took it over to the window seat. Always before she had admired the view from that window and some of its tranquillity would wash over her.

But, with that feeling of restlessness upon her, Mallon could find no tranquillity. Neither could she become involved in her book. She put it down, yet needed something to do.

She went into the bathroom and cleaned her teeth and washed her face, and wished her shower was working. She tried it anyway—

there was no joy, it still wasn't working. Harris had a shower in his bathroom? No! She rejected the idea before it was born. And then remembered that there was a bathroom across the landing.

A minute later and to have a shower suddenly became a must. She went and opened her door and listened. Without any carpets or furnishings to deaden the sound, the faint noise of the television wafted up from the drawing room. Mallon quietly closed her door and without more ado slipped out of her clothes and into her cotton robe. She grabbed up her soap and a towel and in no time went from her room and across the landing, only to find that the bathroom door needed more than a push to open it.

She gave it a thump with her hip—it opened. Closing the door after her, she was soon testing to see if she was getting her hopes up over nothing. Success—the shower was in beautiful working order! In moments she had tied her hair to the top of her head, and was stepping in.

Bliss! Having been deprived of a shower all day, Mallon stood with water cascading over her shoulders for an age before she got busy with the soap. But all good things must come to an end and she finally rinsed the suds away and turned off the shower.

Her thoughts were anywhere as she slid back the shower door prior to stepping out. But as she did step out onto the bathroom floor, so she raised her eyes from watching where she was treading—a must in this never-knew-when-it-was-going-to-jump-up-and-bite-you, hazard-filled house, she had discovered—and she gasped in absolute horror. Because standing there, looking totally thunderstruck, was Harris. She had not a stitch on!

He was shirt and trouser-clad and with a towel thrown over his shoulder. He had obviously just come in and had that moment turned after closing the door after him. For a split second he gazed in stunned fascination at her naked body. Mallon froze. Then, as scarlet colour rioted and seemed to be her only covering, she let out a squeal of anguish and leapt to race past him on her way to the door.

Harris, at once reading her intent, swiftly stepped to the right—out of her way. Unfortunately, Mallon charged to the left, and they collided. He put out a hand to save her, but his touch scalded her, and, her sights set on that door, she pushed him out of the way. She made a lunge for the door—and found it stuck fast!

But, while she was panicking wildly, Harris was getting everything together and had spotted her robe where she had left it. He snatched it up and suddenly he was there at the door with her. 'You're all right, Mallon,' he attempted to soothe her, arranging her robe over her naked shoulders. 'You're safe,' he went on calmly. 'Nothing's going to harm you.' He raised her robe a little and, finding the armholes, 'Put your arms in,' he instructed, but even as—some of her panic starting to fade— she tried to do as he said, it just wasn't happening.

'You try getting wet arms into thin cotton!' she erupted. But, albeit that it wasn't easy, because she insisted on having some of the material to cover up her front when he lent a hand, he made a better job of it than she did. In no time she was covered. He even managed to find the tie belt.

'There,' he said, and Mallon discovered that she must have turned around, because she was suddenly facing him and was looking up into his warm grey eyes. 'All tied up like a Christmas parcel,' he gently teased.

Unbelievably, she found she was smiling, and guessed that that was perhaps his intention. 'I meant to have a word with the plumber. My shower wasn't working this morning,' she explained.

'Neither was mine,' Harris replied, adding, 'When I heard what I thought was your shower in operation, I thought what a good idea, and came to see if this one was in business.' He smiled then, and asked, 'All right now?'

'Y-yes,' Mallon stammered. She was over her shock, but with him so close she was suddenly very much aware of him. 'I'll go,' she said, and turned, ready to give the doorknob another hard tug.

But Harris reached for the doorknob at the same time and, even as he remarked, 'Another job for the carpenters,' and went to move her to one side, he unthinkingly put an arm about her thinly clad shoulders.

The feel of his hand over her hand, the feel of his arm across her shoulders, seemed to cause her to freeze again. She wasn't moving anyway. But supposed that somehow she must have moved—half turned at any rate—towards him. And Harris must have half turned to her too, because all at once they were facing each other again, staring at each other. Staring into one another's eyes.

His hand came away from hers, and she took her hand from the doorknob. 'Mallon.' He murmured her name. Then slowly his head started to come down. Mallon could not have turned from him then had her life depended upon it. And when his mouth met hers, his kiss was what she wanted.

His kiss was gentle, and was over almost as soon as it had begun. But as he broke that gentle kiss he drew her closer to him and, as if he could not resist, he buried his face in her neck. 'You smell wonderful,' he breathed, and while her heart started to beat a crazy rhythm, he pressed his lips to her throat. She felt his grip on her waist tighten momentarily, then Harris was pulling back, straightening up, and taking a pace back. His warm grey eyes studied her deep blue ones and softly he asked, 'Are you going to forgive me for being a mere male?'

Her feelings of panic were a thing of the past, but to be close to Harris like this was sending all sorts of conflicting messages to her. 'I—think I should go,' she decided, her decision very shaky because, staggeringly, she didn't think she wanted to go at all!

'You're not scared of me?' he questioned, his hands falling to his sides.

Mallon felt anything but scared. More, she wanted his hands back on her waist—they'd seemed, just then, to belong there. 'Not at all,' she told him with a smile, and added, perhaps a little less honestly, 'I don't—I mean—I know it was only a small kiss, but I don't want to go any further.' Small kiss! It was blowing her *mind*!

Harris returned her smile and took perhaps another half-step away as he commented, 'Little Mallon Braithwaite—' she'd always thought herself quite tall '—I don't think you've been very far with any man, have you?'

She could have taken exception to his question, but didn't. Suddenly she was feeling happy. And, incredibly, given that she was standing there in her thin robe and nothing else, she felt happy and comfortable with him again—and, once more, able to tell him anything.

'I came close once,' she confessed. And saw he looked interested.

'I do hope, Miss Braithwaite, that, having given me that surprise, you're not going to leave it there.' She laughed. 'When was this?' he wanted to know.

'Oh, a couple of months or so ago.'

'What happened?' Harris persisted.

And Mallon, strangely, now, finding nothing wrong with being dressed the way she was while having this conversation, discovered too that it didn't hurt one tiny bit as she told him, 'He said he loved me. We'd arranged to go away together one weekend. Only at the last minute I couldn't go—so he took my friend instead.'

'Oh, Mallon, you poor love,' Harris murmured.

'Well, she was his friend as well. The three of us worked together.'

'That was your reason for leaving your job?' he questioned, as perceptive as ever. But, no longer smiling, he didn't wait for her to answer but asked abruptly, 'Did you love him?' And, when she did not answer quickly enough, 'Are you still in love with him?' he demanded.

Mallon stared equally solemn-faced at Harris, a gasp of surprise taking her as, like a thunderbolt, it shatteringly at that moment dawned on her why her emotions had been so all over the place just recently. 'No,' she said, and knew it for a certainty. 'I was never in love with him.'

'But, you being you, you must have been extremely fond of him to have contemplated going away with him?'

'It seems ages ago now.' Mallon dismissed the subject lightly, and saw that Harris had taken on board that it was all in her past, dead and buried. 'I'd better go and leave you to your shower,' she said, though she did not want to do anything of the kind.

'Am I allowed to kiss you better before you go?' His good humour appeared to have returned.

Mallon smiled up at him. It didn't hurt— there was nothing to kiss better. Her non-fling with Keith Morgan didn't hurt a bit now, and she was happy. But, because she couldn't help it, and it had been a sort of an invitation anyway, she went forward and stretched up and kissed Harris on his cheek.

Only as she went to pull away Harris, probably thinking to steady her, placed a hand on her ribcage—and she found his touch through the thin material of her robe electric. Their faces were close as they stared at each other, and by mutual consent, naturally, it seemed, they moved together and his mouth was over hers. This time his kiss was nothing like the other two times he had kissed her. It started out gentle and tender, just a meeting of lips, but all at once Mallon was giving in to her need to touch him and, as her arms went around him, so Harris eased her into his arms. As their bodies touched, so his kiss deepened.

Nor did it stay at one kiss. He held her to him, her thin covering no covering at all as he kissed her throat once more, and then again claimed her lips.

'Sweet Mallon,' he murmured, and drew back to look into her eyes. Then, as if he could not resist, 'My dear,' he said softly; and when she was aching for him to kiss her again, her ache was eased when, again, warmly, his kiss intensifying, he lingeringly embraced her again.

Her arms went up and around him when his hands caressed over her back. She loved the feel of his caressing hands, especially when his hands pressed her closer to him.

Tenderly he kissed her throat, tracing kisses up to her ear, one hand caressing to the front of her, moving slowly upwards until gently, gradually, her right breast was captive in his hold.

She leaned her head against his shoulder, his touch as he moulded her breast doing mindless things to her, enchanting her. He kissed her again, his hand lingering, his fingers teasing the hardened nub of her breast.

Then, as if the cotton of her robe was too much of an intrusion, he took his hand from her breast. While holding her close with one arm, while kissing her and seeming to draw the very soul from her as she responded fully, he caressed her spine. Then, while moving, caressing, caressing tenderly up to her throat and down, that hand gently slipped inside her robe.

Mallon felt his sensitive touch capture the naked silken skin of her right breast, and as those sensitive fingers teased at the hardened peak a whole gamut of emotions started to explode within her. She started to sink from the emotion of what he was doing to her, of what he was drawing from her, and a gasp of drowning broke from her.

But her gasp of sound, faint though it had been, reached Harris and he stilled. Although his hand lingered on the wonderful swollen curve of her breast for a second longer, then he reluctantly dragged it across the hardened tip, and finally removed it from her. Then he pulled back to look into her face.

'You're in no danger,' he quietly assured her.

'I...' was about all she could manage as his hands settled on her waist. He straightened up to look searchingly into her disturbed blue eyes, and she was left fighting desperately hard to get herself together. 'I don't want you to kiss me again,' she lied.

'I should think not too,' he answered. 'Disgraceful behaviour.' But he was serious when, allowing some daylight between their two bodies, he said, 'I mean what I said, Mallon—you're safe.'

'I know,' she answered, and turned from him, but was in such a turmoil she had less chance than before of opening the stuck door.

Harris came to the rescue and tugged the door open for her to pass through. 'You're all right, Mallon?' he asked before he let her go.

How could he be so calm when she was such a riot of jangling nerve-ends? 'I'm fine,' she assured him. 'Don't worry.' With that she walked by him and to her bedroom.

Safe? He had aroused such a clamour of out-of-control feelings and emotions in her. But, all too clearly, with that quiet assurance of, 'You're in no danger,' he had been supremely in control of his own feelings and emotions the whole of the time. He had kissed her and she had been emotionally all over the place. But their exchange of kisses had not disturbed him in the slightest! Look how easily he had let her go!

Safe? What was safe about being in love with a man who just did not want to know?

CHAPTER SIX

HARRIS was in her head the moment Mallon awakened on Sunday. She *was* in love with him. It was a fact. It would not go away. The only mystery was—how had it taken so long for her to realise what had been going on inside her? It had started from the first week that she had known him!

Explained, now, were those moments of shyness, of feeling tongue-tied, awkward, but oh, so joyful to see him. This was why she had felt so restless on occasions. This was why… She found herself reliving again his kisses, his touch.

How on earth had she ever imagined that what she felt for Keith Morgan had been love? The fact that he had soon found solace elsewhere when she hadn't been able to go away with him had hurt at the time, but Mallon could only ponder, had it been more hurt pride than anything else? Perhaps she'd experienced a little pain too that he had revealed himself as being fickle and coming from a similar stable to Ambrose and Lee Jenkins.

Whatever, now that she knew the strength of her feelings for Harris—her love for him—Mallon knew that what she had felt for Keith had been nothing remotely like love.

Mallon left her bed to wash and dress, wondering if she had perhaps been looking for an excuse not to go away with Keith that time. She certainly hadn't protested too much when she hadn't been able to go—in fact, she couldn't remember protesting at all.

But Keith Morgan was far from her head when, having to pause first and take a deep breath, Mallon opened her bedroom door.

Sounds below told her that Harris was up and about, and for some seconds she felt such a confusion of emotions, wanting to see him, eager to see him again, yet all of a sudden so overwhelmingly shy to see him, that she just could not move.

But, knowing that she could not stand there dithering all day, she took another deep breath and started off along the landing with no idea of what she would say to Harris. She had last night lyingly told him that she did not want him to kiss her again, but oh, how she had wanted him to kiss her—and to go on kissing her! He had aroused needs and desires in her, and she had wanted to make love with him; had he refused to accept her lie, then she didn't know what would have happened. She hadn't been at all scared; that was one thing she knew for certain.

So how was she supposed to greet him? Was she supposed to just breeze in with a bright Good morning? She could still feel the enrapturing imprint of his caressing hand on her breast, for goodness' sake!

Mallon's dilemma of how she was to greet him, after what to her had been a great degree of intimacy last night, evaporated into nothing when she went into the kitchen. A little too shy to look directly at him for a moment, her eyes went instead to his weekend bag standing on the kitchen table, his car keys next to it!

Dread smote her like a blow. All too plainly, Harris was on the point of departure. 'You don't have to leave because of me!' came blurting from her before she could stop it, her eyes shooting to his.

She wanted to retract the words as soon as they were out, but it was too late. She wanted to run, to hide, but Harris was smiling. 'Because of you?' he queried lightly.

But she knew that he knew quite well what she was referring to, though whether he was teasing her she was too churned up to know. But the fact that they'd had, for the want of better words, an amorous encounter, was out in the open—and Mallon did the only thing left to her. She grinned as she suggested, 'If you promise to never again enter rooms without first knocking, I'll promise to never again prance around n…with nothing on.'

He grinned in return. But then his grin went into hiding, and he was all seriousness when he questioned, 'You slept all right? No—ill effects?'

She hadn't slept so well, but not because she had been worried or afraid. But what she was afraid of now was that if she told him just how unworried and unafraid she had been, she might give away something of how she felt about him.

'Oh, Mallon, my dear,' Harris murmured when she delayed too long in her search for some neutral kind of answer. 'You should have slept soundly. You were never in that sort of jeopardy!'

Had he been trying to calm any fears he thought she might have had, then Mallon did not thank him for it. He was as good as telling her that had she not called a halt to their love-making, then he would have done so. Either that or he was saying that she did not have as much sex appeal as she might think she had!

From another, desperate, pride-backed somewhere, she found another grin. 'That's all right, then,' she answered brightly, not caring at all to be as good as told that she came way down in the desirability stakes. And, just to let him know that she didn't care a hoot whether he went or stayed, 'Anything caustic you want me to tell the plumber tomorrow?'

She dared a glance at Harris and thought she saw a hint of admiration in his eyes at her manner. But she wasn't into trusting her imagination just then—though she all but crumbled when he answered, 'Just tell him that through his negligence the two of us could have got into a great deal of trouble.'

Mallon had to laugh—she rather thought Harris had meant her to. But the next second she didn't feel at all like laughing because he was picking up his bag and car keys. 'Drive safely,' some proud being she was just starting to get to know bade him.

His answer was to come close and drop a light kiss on her cheek in passing. 'Bye,' he said, and went.

How long after he had gone she stood there with her hand pressed against the cheek he had kissed, Mallon didn't know. What she did know was that she, who had never particularly craved other company, was lonely. Not lonely for anyone else—just lonely for Harris.

Somehow she limped through the rest of that day, Harris rarely out of her thoughts. Wasn't love supposed to be joyful? She supposed it would be—if that love were returned. Fate gave a scornful laugh. Fat chance!

On Monday, the plumber sorted the showers out, and her day was brightened on Tuesday when a telephone engineer came to install a telephone. It was a nice surprise. Harris had said nothing about having ordered the service.

That evening Mallon made use of it by ringing her mother and at the same time giving her the telephone number and having a lovely chat. Her mother was extremely happy, and it did Mallon's heart good to hear her sound more bubbly than she could remember her being since Mallon's father had died.

The next few days dragged by, but when Friday arrived Mallon started to feel all agitated inside with anticipation. Harris had driven down last Friday. Perhaps he would drive down today.

She went to bed that night nursing disappointment. She had seen no sign of him, neither had he telephoned. Saturday dawned bright and sunny. Mallon felt pretty much the same. Harris might come today!

But he did not come that day either, nor the next day. The phone stayed silent all weekend, and Mallon endured endless pangs of wanting to see him, and of having him constantly in her head.

The sunny weather turned into a heat wave, and on Monday Mallon started to look forward to the weekend, hoping that, should Harris come down—and surely he must—the weather would hold. She doubted he was able to spend very much time during the week out of doors.

When the builders departed on Monday, she got out the broom and gave the drawing room a sweep and a dust. With the builders hard at their labours, she could have spent her day sweeping and dusting. She was in the drawing room early on Tuesday morning, checking the room over, when for the first time ever the telephone rang—and she all but jumped a mile.

With her heart starting to race, even though she told herself it would be her mother, Mallon went to answer it. 'Hello?' she answered, her voice calm enough. But her heart started to thunder when she recognised her caller's voice.

'Everything going as planned?' Harris enquired coolly.

'No problems,' Mallon replied. She knew she had a smile in her voice—she couldn't help it.

'Good,' he answered, and Mallon, sensing that his call was about to end, desperately wanted to ask if he would be down at the weekend. But couldn't.

'What's your weather doing?' Had she really asked that? Was she so desperate to keep him on the line she was asking about *weather*! 'I expect you're enduring the same heat wave we are.' Shut up! Shut up! 'The joiners have made a lovely job of that piece of banister that needed turning,' she adopted a bright tone to tell him cheerfully. 'Er—did you want to have

a word with Bob? I think he's around somewhere. I can go and find…'

'No need. If you tell me there aren't any
problems, I'm sure it's so,' he answered, and
rang off.

Mallon put down the phone and was in such
an emotional stew that just then she had to be
on her own. The builders were good and gave
her as much privacy as they could, given that
they were in and out of the house the whole
time. She went up to her room and shut herself
away.

Why hadn't she asked him if he was coming
down at the weekend? Or even when he might
next be down? It would have been a perfectly
normal question to have asked, surely?

When she felt she had herself back together
again, Mallon took herself off for a walk,
knowing that her love for Harris had made her
vulnerable. Vulnerable and proud that he
should not see so much as a glimmer of her
feelings for him. So that what had once been
normal was now questioned, just in case she
might be giving herself away.

She returned to Harcourt House. She had
hoped that her walk might make her feel better,
but it had not. What did make her feel better,

however, was to glance out of the kitchen window at lunchtime, just in time to see Harris's car glide by.

Emotional colour immediately flooded her face, so she was glad it would take him a minute or two to get to the kitchen. Hello stranger? No. Today's not Friday or Saturday, is it? No.

Her rehearsed greetings vanished into thin air when, tall, good-looking and with the jacket of his business suit in one hand, Harris walked into the kitchen. 'What are you doing here?' she asked, her heart drumming; she loved him so much! 'Not, of course, that, since you own the place, you can't come and go as you please,' she said lightly, with a small laugh.

Harris did not laugh. In fact there wasn't so much as a smile about him when he stated, 'Talking of problems—I have one I need to discuss with you.'

Alarm instantly filled her. He was going to ask her to leave; she knew that he was! But she didn't want to leave, not now! Not now that she knew she was in love with him. Was that it? Had he seen her love? Was that why he had come personally to tell her to go? Pride suddenly became her ally. He might *think* she was in love with him—she was going to see to it that he had very serious doubts about that.

'I was going to make myself a coffee and a sandwich. Are you in a rush?' she asked pleasantly. It had only been a temporary job anyway. She would tell him that. Should she tell him first that she was leaving before he told her to go? She rather thought that she might.

'A sandwich would be fine,' he answered evenly, and Mallon got out bread, butter, cheese and ham—and reconsidered. She loved him so much; she mustn't be hasty. Perhaps he hadn't come to give her her marching orders. Perhaps... But why...?

She made a plate of sandwiches for them both, but all at once she had no appetite. He draped his jacket over the back of a chair and she made a pot of coffee.

'So what's the problem?' she asked when they were seated at the kitchen table. 'Nothing too serious, I hope.'

Harris placed a sandwich on his plate, and looked across to her. And then said, 'It's Faye.'

Relief drenched her—it didn't sound as if Harris was telling her goodbye. 'Your sister?' she asked, striving to keep her voice level.

He nodded. 'Faye rang me, shortly after I'd phoned you,' he replied. 'It afterwards occurred to me that, if she was passing this way, she might call in to see you.'

Mallon hadn't a clue what he meant by that. Passing this way, Faye would obviously be *en route* to Almora Lodge. But what was Harris saying—that he didn't want his sister to know that Mallon was here at Harcourt House? Was he, after all, asking her to go? 'You couldn't have rung me back and discussed this over the phone?' Mallon asked, her awful feeling of insecurity causing her to go on the attack.

Harris looked at her, his expression solemn. 'It isn't as simple as that,' he replied.

What wasn't? Mallon stared back at him, then all at once something clicked, and, 'Why would your sister call here—to see me?' she asked. And, annoyed suddenly, she exclaimed indignantly, 'You don't want me to tell her what a lecherous swine her husband is. That's it, isn't it? Well, of course I wouldn't!' She was outraged. 'Thanks very much for your high opinion of me!' she snapped.

Only to have her indignation and her feelings of outrage instantly pricked, when Harris replied, 'It's because I hold you in high regard that I've chosen to take time off to come and see you rather than phone.'

Oh, Harris! He held her in high regard! 'Er...' She tried to think clearly. 'So—er—what's the—um—problem?' she asked with what thinking power she had left.

'The problem is that my sister, as clever as she undoubtedly is, is still in love with that low-life she married. I've tried to set her straight—it only made for bad blood between us. So, for the moment, that leaves me having to stand back unable to do anything but just be there to support her as and when I feel called upon to do so.'

Mallon guessed it went very much against the grain for him to stand back, and she could only admire him that, when he must care a lot for his sister, he would do that.

'You—feel the need to support her now about something?' Mallon sifted through what he had said so far, and might be implying.

'The crux of the problem is that Faye, while still hoping to salvage her marriage, got to hear that Phillips has a mistress,' Harris began. 'She had just been in contact with him and was close to being hysterical when she rang me this morning, wanting to know how I could let her down so badly by having her husband's mistress...' He broke off, but was looking directly into Mallon's serious blue eyes when he ended, '...living here in my house.'

'*Me!*' Mallon exclaimed, her mouth falling open in shock. 'He t-told her that *I* was his m-mistress?'

'Incredible, isn't it?'

Mallon was very near speechless. 'The reptile!' she gasped, and then recalled the last time she had seen Roland Phillips. 'I did this!' she blurted out.

'You did this?' Harris challenged—and she rushed on.

'He's paying me back. I saw him...'

'When?' Harris cut aggressively through what she was saying. 'When did you see him? Has he been here again?' he demanded.

'No!' Mallon answered. 'It was—er—the other Saturday.'

'The day after I told him not to come here again?'

Mallon nodded. 'I'd gone for a walk. I think to prove to myself that I wasn't scared.'

'I remember,' Harris inserted, his tone quieter. He continued to be gentle as he asked, 'How did you feel when you saw him?'

She smiled then. 'Not scared,' she answered. 'What I was, was angry. I got stroppy anyway and told him I found him totally repulsive and something to the effect that, were it not for the fact of telling him that if he ever came near me again I would report him to the police, I wouldn't lower myself to speak to the likes of him.'

'You did that?' Harris asked, and she basked for a moment in what she thought was admiration in his eyes. But his expression was changing as he questioned, 'How have you been sleeping?'

With Harris so much in her head, the fact that she loved him so much but that he would never love her, badly, was her answer. 'I haven't had one single, solitary bad dream since, if that's what you're asking,' she replied. 'But we're digressing. Naturally, should your sister call, I would most definitely let her know that I'm not her husband's mistress. I'll...'

'You won't have to,' Harris interrupted. But, oddly then, he paused for a moment before he added, 'I've already convinced her of that.'

Normally Mallon would have accepted that, and would perhaps have said something to the effect that that was all right, then. But something—maybe something in his pause—perhaps something in her heightened sensitivity to him—had her questioning.

'And—she believed you? Just like that?' They were talking here of a woman who was very much in love with her husband. Would Faye, no matter how much of a rat that man might be, believe, with no evidence, that the woman her husband had said was his mistress was not—purely on her brother's say so? Particularly as the said mistress was living only a few miles up the road from him? 'How?' Mallon asked. 'How did you convince her?'

'Ah,' Harris murmured, and Mallon instinctively knew she was not going to like his answer, whatever it was. Her instinct was proved right, even if he did preface it with, 'As I mentioned, Faye was close to being hysterical. The only way I could think to calm her down was to tell her that you were not *his* girlfriend—but mine.'

Mallon stared at him staggered. 'Mistress!' she exploded. 'You said *mistress*! You told your sister I was your m...' She couldn't believe it. 'What else did you tell her that she was likely to believe?' she questioned with sharp sarcasm, her eyes flashing sparks.

Harris met her angry gaze full on, but did not duck from answering. 'I tried to keep as near to the truth as possible,' he owned.

'Oh, it sounds like it!' she flared hostilely.

'I was wrong. I know I was wrong. But she was hurting—I've sort of got used to picking her up and making her feel better when she's fallen down. It's second nature to me, I suppose.'

Mallon felt herself beginning to soften. She made herself toughen up. He was outrageous! What he had told his sister was outrageous. 'So?' Mallon questioned belligerently.

'So I told her you had worked for Phillips for a few weeks, mainly when he was out of the country. That you had walked out on him when he'd come home and made a pass at you.'

Well, that was true. 'Go on,' Mallon invited stonily.

'I said I was driving by and, as you didn't have transport, offered you a lift to the station, but that before we got there I offered you a job here and—um—things went on from there.'

'Just as if I was any sort of—fl-floozie, who'd hop into bed with any…'

'Of course not!' Harris cut her off sharply.

'Not much!' Mallon cried, and, starting to get too stewed up to sit still any longer, she shot to her feet—and so did he. As toe to toe they faced each other, she erupted again, 'Then—after your phone call—you realised that your sister might belt down here to have it out with her husband, and that she might also take it into her head to call in here and say hello to me. And you couldn't have that, so you hot-footed it down here…'

'I wanted to tell you personally. I…'

'You have!' Mallon snapped, and, too het up suddenly to stay talking to him, she announced angrily, 'I'm going for a walk!' She was over by the door when she threw over her shoulder, 'I hope, if you've any decency, that you'll be gone by the time I get back!'

She set off at a brisk pace, but within five minutes the heat of the day caused her to slow down. She was still angry with Harris, though. Why couldn't he have told his sister the truth? So, okay, Faye had been hysterical, but who did Harris Quillian think he was, telling his sister that she was his mistress? Even if his sister was hurting quite desperately and in urgent need to know that by no chance was he housing her husband's mistress.

The thought of Faye Phillips's dreadful hurt weakened Mallon a little. Poor Faye. She had been hoping to be reconciled with her husband—but, by the look of it, he didn't want to know. Mallon pushed such weakening thoughts away from her. She wanted to stay angry. Even if Harris Quillian had grown up looking out for his sister, that still didn't give him the right to go round telling her what he had—even if it had calmed her and made her feel a little better.

Mallon had walked for about a mile when she realised she was feeling calmer herself. She even began to wonder what she had got so stewed up about? True, she didn't want to be thought of as any man's mistress, but, it was only a name after all. *She* knew she wasn't. *He* knew she wasn't, and, oh, hang it—she'd said she hoped he'd be gone by the time she got back.

Mallon turned about, trying not to see the funny side of it. It was his house, when all was said and done. He could come and go as he pleased—and she had more or less ordered him out!

She made her way back to Harcourt House knowing that, while inwardly she might still be a little angry with him, that she might not even like him very much just then, she still loved the swine. If he had gone, heaven alone knew when she might see him again.

There was a car on the drive Mallon did not recognise when she reached Harcourt House. She took little notice of it. With so many expert tradesmen about there seemed always to be some different car or other parked about. Anyhow, there was only one car she was interested in seeing.

It was still there. She breathed a sigh of relief—and could afford to be angry again. Harris must have heard her coming along the hall, for he suddenly appeared from the drawing room.

Her intention to turn into the kitchen without a word was thwarted, however, when Harris smilingly called, 'I'm glad you're back. We have a visitor.'

Mallon halted, the smart-looking car on the drive and her earlier spat with Harris and its contents merging with that 'We have a visitor', and starting to mean something.

'How nice!' she answered pleasantly, unsure how sharp Faye Phillips's ears were—if Harris Quillian was waiting for a smile, though, he'd have a long wait. She went towards him, but was glad he had the sense not to put an arm across her shoulders as he escorted her to the drawing room.

A tall dark-haired woman, about ten years younger than Harris, was standing watching the door when they went in. 'You must be Mallon,' she said. For all she smiled her greeting, Mallon thought Faye looked sad and vulnerable and, if she wasn't mistaken, just a little red around the eyes, as if she had recently been crying.

Harris introduced them and Mallon smiled brightly, and said, 'Hello,' adding, 'I'm sorry I wasn't here when you arrived. I popped out for a walk.'

'While I did a building inspection,' Harris slipped in.

'I should have let you know I was stopping by,' Faye said apologetically to Mallon, hesitated, and then added, 'You've probably guessed I've been to see Roly.'

'I thought perhaps you might.' Mallon could see no point in pretending otherwise. But, not wanting Harris's sister to dwell on something that had clearly been, and still was, very painful to her, 'Have you eaten? I can get you…'

'I couldn't eat a thing.' Faye Phillips smiled.

'But you don't have to dash back, I hope?' From what Mallon could see, the woman was in need of large doses of TLC.

'Oh, that's kind of you. The setting here is so tranquil.'

'You must stay as long as you like,' Harris invited.

'Are you sure?' Faye turned to Mallon and confided, 'I feel a bit of a wreck, actually. While I do have a meeting in London early tomorrow morning, I wouldn't mind at all relaxing down here overnight. Would that be all right with you, Mallon?' she asked. 'Harris mentioned about a month ago that, albeit undecorated and minimally furnished, he now has two bedrooms just about habitable.'

Mallon's thoughts were quickly into how she would give her Harris's room, when he answered his sister's question for her. 'Of course you must stay. You'll be able to get to know each other. You'd like that, wouldn't you, Mallon?' he asked.

'I'd be delighted to have your company,' Mallon assured Faye, knowing she had no option and hoping that, since Faye knew of her employment with Roland Phillips and her 'involvement' with Harris, she'd barely have to be on her guard, if at all.

Which would all have been fine but for two things: Harris checking his watch and commenting generally, 'I shall shortly have to think about getting back to London,' and his sister objecting strongly to the idea.

'Oh, you can't!' she cried.

'I can't?' he queried, with a brother's teasing expression on his face.

'You've come down to be with Mallon. I shall feel dreadful if you go back because I'm here,' she wailed. 'I can have the spare room, can't I, Mallon? And...' Her voice tailed off. The unhappy woman looked so near to tears again that Mallon couldn't bear it, because it seemed to her that Faye had probably got an overnight bag with her and had hoped, expected, to be staying overnight at Almora Lodge.

'Certainly you can,' she declared cheerfully, and looked at Harris, fully expecting him to gently insist that he had business in London that just would not wait.

But, to her utter astonishment, 'We can't have Faye feeling like that, can we, Mallon? It looks as though matters financial in London will have to wait.'

Mallon was still staring at him uncomprehendingly when Faye said that, since they hadn't known she was coming, the room wouldn't be ready, and began to insist on making up the bed herself. Only then did it dawn on Mallon that, while other bedrooms in the house were in the process of being replastered, they were nowhere near ready for anyone to sleep in them.

Even while she was quickly mentally switching Faye over to have the one habitable guest room—her room—Mallon was startlingly realising that there was only *one* other bed in the house!

Her eyes shot to Harris, but from the way he stared urbanely back she knew that he had also done the two-beds-divided by-three-people calculation. 'I wouldn't dream of letting you.' She found she was answering Faye's insistence to make up her own bed. But, very much aware that Faye thought she and her brother slept together, Mallon still expected Harris to intervene. When he did no such thing, Mallon started to get angry. Though bearing in mind that the best way to convince Faye that she was not her husband's mistress was to let her believe she shared a bed with Harris, Mallon managed to hide her anger by adding, 'Though since I'm hot and sticky from my walk, and need a shower, I wouldn't mind if one of you nipped out to the supermarket for me.'

'I'll go,' Faye offered at once. But before Mallon could begin to wind up to what she would say to one Mr Harris Quillian, once the two of them were alone, he was offering to go to into town to the supermarket with his sister.

'Perhaps you'd like to give me a list,' he suggested.

She'd like to give him a punch on the head! Mallon concocted a list and handed it to him. He glanced at the first item and his lips twitched and Mallon again felt the need for physical violence. He thought the first item— 'I hate you, Quillian'—was funny!

'We'll go now,' he told his sister, and as Faye took a step towards the door so Harris came over to Mallon and bending down, on the pretext of kissing her cheek, he breathed in her ear, 'Promise you'll still be here when I get back?'

Her insides felt all wobbly at the firm hold of his hands on her arms, at the touch of his wonderful mouth against her cheek. Though, from some stronger somewhere, she managed to grit beneath her breath, 'Don't tempt me!' As he stepped back, she smiled at Faye. 'Bye.'

Mallon stood motionless for a minute or two after they had gone. It was, she admitted, tempting to leave. That monster Quillian didn't deserve any better. Against that, though, and aside from the fact that she had nowhere else to go if she didn't want to go and park herself on her mother and John, she still loved the monster.

Leaving the drawing room, Mallon went up the stairs to survey the two habitable bed-rooms. She had no intention of sharing a bed-room with him, though—she just couldn't. She remembered her responses to him that Saturday when he had come for a shower just after she'd had hers. No! It was impossible.

She wouldn't! She couldn't. If he kissed her again…! Stop it! Why would he kiss her again? Get your head together, do.

Mallon started work on the two rooms. But, even as she worked, she knew it wouldn't come to sharing a room with him. There was no mistaking his sister's look of vulnerability, but she had seemed reasonably calm—well, certainly not hysterical, as Harris said she had been when she had phoned him. Perhaps, while they were out, Harris would tell Faye the truth of their arrangement here. Perhaps he would tell her that she was his caretaker and nothing more than that.

But Faye was hurting, was hurting very badly. What better way to convince her that she did have his total support, that he was not housing her husband's mistress? What better way to convince her…?

Mallon took her toiletries out from the one bathroom and transferred them, along with some of her belongings, into the next-door bedroom and bathroom. Any items remaining in the wardrobe and drawers could, she felt, quite understandably be put down to her spreading out while waiting for the bedrooms to be fully furnished.

Making up both beds with fresh linen, Mallon became more and more sure that Harris would have come up with a pretty good explanation while he and Faye were out. Though the weakening thought did start to creep in that, if the worst did come to the worst and she did have to share a room with him, then, since the weather was so hot, and nobody would want many clothes on the bed, he could have the duvet for a mattress on the floor.

But she quickly cancelled that soft-hearted thought; it wouldn't come to that. While it was true that Faye was distressed and must inwardly be hurting dreadfully—and it was also true that Harris was doing the very best he could to take care of her—Mallon started to grow more and more confident that, by the time they returned, he would have told Faye all that there was to tell her.

Perhaps they'd have a laugh about it before he went back to London, Mallon mused when at last she was able to take a shower, though since she was using Harris's bathroom she first locked the door. She even smiled to herself, knowing that she had been worrying needlessly. In fact, so certain did she become that she had nothing at all to worry about, she determined that, once she'd finished her shower, she would set about moving everything back into her own room.

Once she had dried off and changed into fresh underwear and a fresh dress, though, she remembered that Kevin usually called in at the kitchen around now. Ostensibly to fill his kettle, but in reality looking for a cup of tea.

She was half minded to let him make his own tea, but he was such a willing lad and was always pleased to give her a lift in the van to anywhere she wanted to go. So, instead of moving her belongings back to her own room, she went downstairs to make Kevin a cup of tea.

The tea was just made when Harris's car went past the kitchen window. 'Here comes the boss,' Kevin announced. 'I'll take my tea outside, then I'll go and see how my horses have done.' Kevin liked his daily small flutter on the races. 'Want anything bringing back?' he asked.

'Not today,' she answered with a smile, and was pouring his tea when Harris and his sister appeared with plastic carriers of shopping.

As Kevin took his tea with him, Mallon looked to Harris and Faye. They were not smiling as if about to tell her that all had been revealed, and Mallon waited.

'Harris said you liked flowers.' Faye found a smile, and handed her a lovely bouquet of yellow roses.

'Thank you. Aren't they beautiful!' Mallon exclaimed, taking them from her. She waited. Still nothing. 'I've made some tea,' she announced.

'Shall I get my overnight bag in first?' Faye asked, confirming for Mallon that the poor woman had half anticipated that she would be staying overnight at Almora Lodge.

'You didn't tell her?' Mallon challenged as soon as Faye Phillips was out of earshot.

'Tell her?'

Mallon had a momentary, and joyful, vision of Quillian with a cauliflower ear. She controlled herself. 'Why can't you tell Faye the truth about…?'

'About Phillips? You'd like me to tell her that her husband, the man she is so besotted with, assaulted you, tore your clothing, and the devil alone knows what he would have attempted had you not been able to get away?' he challenged harshly. 'You can see how she is now. What do you think it would do to her to know that?'

Mallon's anger faded into nothing. 'You don't think she has an idea what he's capable of?' she questioned in a half-hearted attempt not to be defeated.

'I strongly suspect that she has,' he answered. 'But she's heard as much about him just lately as she can take. I honestly don't think she's up to taking much more. I've done what I can—she has to sift through everything now in her own quiet time.'

'And will she?'

'She will. She has a fine brain. I don't think she's far off realising that she's been totally blinkered where Phillips is concerned.' Harris looked seriously at Mallon when he added, 'Faye and I came close to being enemies when she wouldn't listen to my telling her some truths about him. I've since had to swallow down my natural instincts and go along with her because...'

'Because you need her to know you'll be there to support her when the scales finally fall from her eyes,' Mallon cut in without thinking.

'Oh, Mallon, you understand so well,' he murmured, and, when she had quite forgotten why she had been angry with him, or, in fact, that she had ever been angry with him at all, he added softly, 'In fact, my dear, as well as being beautiful on the outside, you have an inner beauty that hits me time and time again.'

Mallon stared at him, her heart racing. Did he really think that about her? She felt weak at the knees. But then quickly realised that, whether he did or whether he didn't, it was still miles away from him being in love with her. If she didn't want him to know what effect his words had on her, then she had better get her act together—and be sharp about it!

'So where did you suppose you might be sleeping tonight?' she asked pithily.

Harris looked at her, annoying her afresh that, instead of being put out, there actually seemed to be a hint of humour in his grey eyes. 'Ah, Mallon, you wouldn't have me sleep in my car, would you?' he asked.

She smiled the sweetest smile. 'Of course not,' she answered nicely, and, her sweet tone fading, she retorted, 'For preference I'd have you sleep in a ditch!' He had just burst out laughing when his sister returned. Mallon transferred her attention to Faye. 'Your room's all ready, I'll come up with you, if you like, while Harris puts the shopping away.'

Against all the odds, dinner that evening—chicken and vegetables with custard tart, and cheese and biscuits to follow—was a surprisingly pleasant meal. Mallon could only put the fact that the meal seemed so without strain of any sort down to the fact that all three of them were making an effort.

She knew that *she* was making an effort. In her empathy with Faye she had bottled down her tremendous inner disquiet about having to share a room with Harris. She had searched and searched for alternatives, and in truth had come up with many: drawing room sofa, duvet on floor of one of the uninhabitable bedrooms, even putting the duvet in the bath—though, bearing in mind how tall Harris was, Mallon couldn't see herself putting him through that.

Faye too was making every effort, chatting cheerfully, responding brightly to the flow of conversation Harris instigated time and again. If occasionally her eyes clouded over in moments of forgetfulness of her surroundings, and that heartbreaking vulnerability showed through, then Faye seemed to recollect where she was and returned to being bright and cheerful again.

And Harris, Mallon had to concede, was a super person to have at the dinner table. Bearing in mind that he knew both her frailties and his sister's, he was charming and witty, so that by the end of the meal Mallon, if not forgetting her worries, had to some extent put them to the back of her mind.

Those worries came rushing to the fore, however, once the meal was over and the used dishes were in the dishwasher and everything was once more spick and span. The three of them had moved to the drawing room with a suggestion that they watch some television. But Faye appeared to have too much going on in her head to be able to sit watching the small screen.

'If no one minds, I think I'll go to bed,' she said, getting to her feet. 'I've an early start in the morning,' she excused.

'Would you like a warm drink to take up with you?' Mallon offered.

'No, but thank you all the same,' Faye declined. However, she found a smile as she in return offered, 'Since I shall be away so early, I'll bring you a cup of tea up before I go.' And while Mallon was making a mental note to be up before the birds in the morning, Faye wished her and Harris goodnight and, closing the drawing room door after her, she went up to her room.

Mallon knew all about being unable to settle to watch television. Five minutes later she gave up all pretence of trying to concentrate on the programme. She turned to look at Harris, and found he wasn't watching the television at all, but was watching her.

Without more ado he got up and switched the television set off. Then he came and stood looking down at her. 'You'll be all right with me, Mallon.' He'd brought out into the open the worries which had been stewing away inside of her.

'Do I have to?' she blurted out. 'I mean, is it strictly necessary for—for you to share my room?'

'Can you think of an alternative?' he asked in return, ignoring that in actual fact she would be sharing *his* room, the one he used whenever he came down to Harcourt House.

'You obviously can't,' she replied, realising that he must have searched as hard as she had

for a solution that wouldn't upset his sister—
she was upset enough already.

'You've been so good about all this,' Harris
stated warmly. 'It seems poor recompense that
you should have to share that bed with me.
P...'

'Hold it right there, Quillian!' Mallon
erupted, and was on her feet. 'Who said anything about sharing the bed?' It gave her the
greatest pleasure to be able to tell him, 'You
can have the duvet—it might help to soften
those hard floorboards.'

Her small feeling of triumph never breathed
life. The least she'd expected was a scowl;
what she got was a laugh. 'Heartless wench!'
he called her nicely. But, as he came close up
to her and looked deep into her lovely eyes,
he was unsmiling as he assured her seriously,
'You're safe with me, Mallon. I'm not like
Phillips, or your ex-boyfriend, or any other li-
centious male of your acquaintance.'

Mallon rather thought she knew that.
'You're still sleeping on the floor!' she
snapped, and thought that to follow Faye's example and go upstairs was a very good idea.
'Goodnight!' she bade him shortly, and went
at speed. If he answered, she didn't hear him.

In his room, which for that night she now regarded as hers, Mallon quickly showered and got into her nightdress. After listening for sounds that might indicate Faye was wandering around, and on hearing none, Mallon tossed the duvet off the bed and onto the floor. Looking at the jumbled heap, conscience made her go over and spread it out. She tested it with her hands. The floor felt rock-hard! Even with the rug she then went and placed under it it was barely any better. She toughened her soft heart—he still wasn't going to share her bed.

After placing a pillow on the floor, Mallon climbed into bed, a solitary sheet on that hot night her only covering. She lay down, but was still awake at one in the morning. Harris definitely wasn't going to share her bed—he hadn't come up the stairs yet.

An hour later, when she had started to form the view that he must have decided to sleep on the sofa in the drawing room—perhaps with the intention of telling Faye that they'd had cross words or something—Mallon's ears, alert for every sound, heard Harris almost silently enter the bedroom.

The only light in the room was from the moonlit sky and the illuminated dial on the bedside clock, but, even so, Mallon closed her eyes and concentrated on making her breathing sound regular. She was overwhelmingly aware of him quietly moving around and was glad as his eyes became accustomed to the darkness that he found his 'floor bed' without bumping into anything.

'Goodnight,' he said, to let her know he knew she was awake. She didn't answer—but went to sleep with a smile on her face.

Mallon awoke feeling cold. She glanced at the clock and saw that it was ten past three. She looked over to where Harris was. She was cold—and he'd got the duvet. She heard him. He was restless; she guessed the floor was getting harder by the second.

Ten minutes later he was still restless, and she knew couldn't be asleep. She had gone from feeling cold to feeling thoroughly chilled. She wondered if he was cold too.

Oh, this was ridiculous! 'Give me your pillow,' she commanded.

She'd said it quietly, just in case he was asleep. But a moment later his pillow landed. Mallon got out of bed and placed his pillow at the foot of the bed. Then she went and got into bed under the sheet.

She swallowed, her courage failing her. Then she shivered and her brain decided this was all completely crackers—she trusted him, for goodness' sake. 'Your pillow's at the bottom of the bed if you want to share the duvet,' she said in a low tone, not wanting to wake Faye, should the poor woman be asleep.

Mallon heard Harris move, then the duvet came over her. His shape loomed out of the semi-darkness but, just when she was about to have second thoughts about the wisdom of what she had done, Harris, his voice threatening, warned her, 'You lay one finger on me, Mallon Braithwaite, and I'll yell the house down!'

What could she do? She stifled a laugh, then didn't feel at all like laughing as his bare leg made contact with her bare leg. 'On *top* of the sheet!' she ordered on a hiss of sound.

'Sorry, your honour,' he answered, and dutifully complied.

She loved him, and started to feel less cold. When she started to actually feel warm, Mallon went to sleep. She awoke with a start to find that dawn had broken and that two things seemed to have simultaneously brought her awake. One, the sound of teacups tinkling in saucers, the other, the feel of Harris moving to get under the sheet with her—not at the bottom of the bed, where he should have been, but at the top!

'*Get…*' was as far as she managed to shriek before Harris clamped a hand over her mouth, silencing her. She wriggled violently to get away, her bare—*bare?*—thigh brushing against his bare thigh.

'Faye's at the door with the tea tray!' Harris hurriedly whispered.

Mallon fumed impotently as he took his hand away. But, unused to being found in bed with anybody, Mallon couldn't take it, and as Faye tapped softly on the door and came in, so Mallon ducked her head beneath the covers.

The side of her face brushed against Harris's hair-roughened chest and, while she realised he was naked from the waist up, she hoped with all she had that he was wearing *something*!

'I'd make a useless waitress!' She heard Faye laugh as she apologised for spilling tea into the saucers. But whatever Harris said in reply Mallon didn't catch—her attention was suddenly riveted elsewhere as she realised that with one hand splayed against Harris's chest, as though to push him away, her fingers were touching his right nipple.

'You'll be all right?' she heard Harris ask his sister, but Mallon didn't hear what Faye said this time. Somehow, as if fascinated, Mallon found that her forefinger was exploring his nipple.

She traced the circle of it, the tip of it, and had the most wild notion all at once to put her lips to it. She wouldn't, though. Not with Faye in the same room. But, come to think of it, wouldn't it be safer to do that while Faye was there?

Moments later and suddenly some devilment seemed to come alive in Mallon. After all, this situation was none of her making. She moved her head, her lips parting as she came into contact with Harris's nipple. She kissed it. Kissed it again. Touched it again. And then took the tip inside her lips. All at once she found pleasure in playing with his nipple, the tip of her tongue finding it totally fascinating. She kissed it, and teased at it with her tongue and lips.

Indeed, so taken up was she with what she was doing that a gasp of shock left her when, abruptly, the covers were pulled back from her head and, 'Just what do you think you're do-ing?' Harris enquired quietly. As, abruptly, any remaining feeling of devilment Mallon had ex-perienced promptly departed.

'Wh-where's Faye?' she asked shakily.

'On her way back to London by now, I shouldn't wonder.'

'Oh. Um—sorry.' Mallon apologised for making free with his nipple. Then thought, Hang on here—it was her space that had been intruded upon. 'I just thought I'd pay you—um—back a little.' She excused what she only then started to realise was out-and-out wanton-ness.

Harris was lying on his side and stared down at her. 'And how would you feel if I did done the same to you?' he questioned and while her colour flared and her heartbeats started to race, 'Sorry,' he apologised. 'I couldn't resist that. One of us had better get up.'

They both went to leap out of bed at the same time—and collided. Her nightdress must have ridden up during her sleep and she felt the length of his bare thighs against her.

'Oh,' she cried—but it wasn't a wail of panic.

Though she supposed that there must have been a hint of panic in there somewhere, because Harris was gently calming her, 'Hush, you're all right,' while at the same time backing his body from her.

Mallon looked up at him and somehow had the weirdest feeling that she didn't want to be all right. 'I'm not worried,' she told him honestly.

'You're sweet,' he said, and smiled, and moved a little further back. Though, prior to leaving the bed, he went to place a light kiss on the end of her nose. Only, intending to back away too, she moved as well—and somehow their lips met.

It was a brief meeting of their two mouths, and they both pulled back, staring into each other's eyes. The next Mallon knew was that she had moved forward and so had Harris—and unexpectedly she found herself in his arms.

It was where she longed to be, and she could not help but put her arms around him, and as he held her close, so she moved closer still. She felt him burying his head in her neck, in her hair, and then she felt his mouth on hers again, gently seeking this time; seeking, finding, gently giving, gently taking as her lips parted.

She loved him so, and that love seemed to consume her as, with gentle tender hands, she caressed his broad shoulders. Again Harris kissed her, trailing kisses down her throat. 'You're exquisite,' he murmured, and she thrilled at his words, at this closeness.

She wanted to be closer to him still and dared to move that little bit nearer, feeling his warmth, feeling his hard chest against her breasts.

When Harris drew back to look into her face she could do nothing but smile, her lips parting, inviting his kisses.

Oh, my darling, she thought, enraptured when, accepting that invitation, his head came down again and he kissed her. She felt his hands at her back, caressing, moving round to the front, caressing still, this time searching.

His left hand found her right breast, and she sighed from the pure pleasure of his touch. 'Oh!' she sighed, enchanted, and kissed him and held him close. As their kiss broke, so his sensitive fingers moved up to the tiny pearl buttons of her nightdress, unhurriedly unfastening.

Returning again to her mouth, his kisses became more passionate. She felt his hands caress the nakedness of her breasts and, as her heart leapt, she smiled shyly up at him in full agreement to his touch. She pressed closer to him, uncaring then of anything but her love for him and the magic of desire he was drawing from her. She wanted him, it was that simple, and she had not the smallest objection to make when he slid her nightdress from her shoulders and down past her waist.

He held her closely to him then, the broad expanse of his naked chest against her swollen breasts, kissing her deeply for long ageless seconds. 'Sweet Mallon,' he murmured, caressing her—and Mallon never wanted him to stop.

More, when he kissed her breasts, first one, then the other, his gentle fingers circling the hardened tips in much the same way her finger had circled his nipple, he evoked in her an untamed need for him.

Then Harris was lying over her and Mallon thrilled at this new closeness, her hands going to his waist, to the material of his shorts. More enchantment was hers when his hands moved her nightdress yet further down and away from her. She felt the thrill of his tender touch as he caressed her naked buttocks and, her heart in overdrive, she wanted to know more of his skin too, wanted to place her hands inside the back of his shorts and press him to her.

She wanted him. More and more she wanted him. 'Harris.' She spoke his name huskily, wanting him so badly, yet at the same time feeling suddenly shy.

'Mallon?' he responded to the unspoken question in her voice.

'I—um...' She didn't want to talk; she wanted to kiss him. So she kissed him and, because this was such new territory for her, she pulled back to look at him, and smiled as she told him, 'I—um—think I'm in need of a little guidance here,' and immediately wished she hadn't.

Because as Harris lay over her—looked down at her, feasted his eyes on her face with her thick blonde hair all tousled around her head—he all at once stilled, glanced away from her; and then groaned an agonised kind of groan.

'What did I say—do?' she asked, completely bewildered.

But Harris had moved from her and was lying on his stomach, his face in the pillow. 'I said you'd be safe,' he groaned. She didn't want to be safe.

'That's…'

'Mallon, don't talk. Just do me a favour.' Anything. Anything at all. 'Get out of bed— now,' he requested through what seemed to be clenched teeth.

'G-get out…'

'*Now!*' he repeated urgently. But she didn't want to. She wanted him. She loved him. She wanted his hold, his touch. She wanted to be held in love for just a while.

That was when reality, cold reality, which she didn't want, started to force its terrible way in. Hang on here—Harris didn't love her. He had never pretended that he did. The love was all on her side!

'*Please*, Mallon,' he urged, his tone strained. 'Go now!'

Mallon drew a shaky breath. She still did not want to go. But Harris wanted her to go. He didn't love her. The love was all on her side. Mallon stirred and, dragging herself away from him, got out of bed.

'Consider it done,' she managed croakily—and fled.

She reached her room, her head in a whirl. She knew that she could trust him. But what rocked her, and shook her to her foundations, was that nobody had told her that she shouldn't trust herself!

CHAPTER SEVEN

THAT phrase was still rocking her minutes later when Mallon stood beneath the shower and tried to get her head together. *She could trust him—but she couldn't trust herself.* Oh, Harris, Harris, what had he done to her? Her body still ached for him and, had he not told her to go…

Mallon was still trying to get herself into more of one piece when, dried and dressed, she had to face the most unpalatable truth—it was time to leave. Oh, how she did not want to go. But oh, how she recognised that go she must.

She knew she had been in a bit of a state when she had first come to Harcourt House—it seemed Roland Phillips made a practice of going around wrecking women's lives—but she was all right now. And she had Harris to thank for that. Just as he was doing all that he could for his sister, he had invented a job for the bedraggled wretch he had seen walking along in the pouring rain, and in doing so had begun a healing process for her.

So, fine, she had made Harcourt House a little more liveable-in than it had been, but her continued presence here was not, strictly speaking, necessary. Should there be a delivery of more furniture or carpets, or anything at all, then there were always at least four men on site who could direct delivery people.

It was with a deep sadness in her heart that, having already delayed as long as she could, Mallon left her room. She had so many mixed feelings about seeing Harris again. Yet, if she was to leave and never to see him again after that, she so desperately needed to see him now—just the one more time.

A kind of panic hit her then that, for all she hadn't heard his car, Harris might have already left! Hurrying up her steps, she went down the stairs and into the kitchen. His car was outside—and so was he. Oh, heavens, it was still early, but he appeared to be on the point of leaving.

Mallon swallowed hard. She badly wanted to go out to him—she could tell him she was leaving—but suddenly she felt too paralysed to move. Then she saw Harris take a glance to the kitchen window. He saw her, and started to move. He was coming back in.

Oh, grief! While wanting so desperately to hide, Mallon also quite desperately needed some contact with him. His expression when he entered the kitchen was almost stern. But as Harris looked across at her, he smiled suddenly. 'You okay, Mallon?' he asked.

Devastated, if you want to know. 'Absolutely,' she answered brightly.

Her insides were already in a giant upheaval, but that was before Harris went on to bring out into the open what her suddenly pinkened skin was all about! 'You know that our—um-bed-share—was never meant to end that...' He broke off, and it seemed to her that, when Harris was usually so confident about everything, this time he was having to search to find the right words. 'Have I harmed you?' he asked abruptly, his smile gone.

Oh, Harris! Her heart went out to him for his sensitivity. 'Not a bit!' she assured him. 'Other than...'

'Other than?' he quickly took up, his searching grey eyes scrutinising her face.

'Other than you've restored my faith in men.' She felt she owed him that honesty.

'*I* have?' he exclaimed in surprise.

She hadn't wanted to mention the amorous time they had shared. Indeed, had she been asked, she would have said she'd have sprinted like crazy away from doing so. But she had learned of Harris's sensitivity, and it seemed to her then that he was blaming himself for what had happened when she knew full well that, by taking liberties with his person—albeit that she'd started them only to pay him back— *she* had been the instigator.

So she took a brave breath and told him openly, 'You taught me this morning that not all men are like my former stepfather or his son, or Keith Morgan or Roland Phillips. And...'

'Oh, Mallon—does that mean you really do trust me?'

'Of course,' she answered without hesitation, and smiled. But, while being so open with him, she could not be so open as to tell him of the shattering truth she had discovered— that it was herself she did not trust. 'It was my fault,' she freely admitted. 'Though I fully intended to be up bright and early.'

'As did I,' Harris chipped in. 'Blame it on the previous sleepless hours that, were it not for the rattling teacups, I'd probably still be asleep now. As it is, I can't tell you how sorry I am that I—overstepped the mark.'

She wanted to say something light, a Think nothing of it would have done, but the words got stuck in her throat. So she drew breath to tell him what she had to tell him. 'Harris, I...' Was as far as she got, because, almost as if he knew what she had been preparing to say, he interrupted her.

'This won't make any difference?' he asked.

'Difference?'

'You wouldn't dream of leaving me?'

Oh, Harris! She was weak. She knew she was weak. Even as she knew that he wasn't asking about her leaving him, but about leaving his employ, Mallon was listening to her heart and not her head.

And, 'What sort of a girl do you take me for?' she answered lightly.

'You'll stay?'

'Of course.'

He looked relieved. 'Good,' he said, and looked about to come over and kiss her cheek. But he checked himself, and instead said, 'I'd better get off.' Giving her a warm smile, he turned about.

Mallon collapsed onto a kitchen chair once he had gone. She was weak, pathetic, and should have told him that she wasn't staying. But she loved him—and that seemed to have stripped away her backbone.

Anyhow, this job had never been permanent, she argued to her name-calling self. So surely she wasn't being all *that* spineless when any week now she would have to face doing what today she had put off doing.

She set the kettle to boil ready for when Bob Miller arrived, but her thoughts were far from making a pot of tea and more to do with the fact that the last time Harris had left he had kissed her cheek. This time, maybe to try and reassure her that she had nothing to fear, he hadn't come anywhere near.

Mallon spent the next two days knowing what she already knew anyway, that she did not fear anything about Harris. He was in her head the whole of the time. He was there in her thoughts when she got up in the morning, there when she went to bed at night.

She rang her mother, and had quite a long chat—and Harris was still there. She thought of him while she chatted to the workmen, when she went to Sherwins in the van with

Kevin. In fact there was little room in her head for anyone but Harris.

It just wasn't good enough, she told herself countless times. She shouldn't be spending her days just dwelling on thoughts of him. She should be thinking of looking for a career. Thinking in terms of what she would do when she left Harcourt House as, inevitably, she would have to.

The trouble was that she couldn't think of a career. She had no idea what she wanted to do apart from stay somewhere near Harris for the rest of her life. Pathetic? Pathetic wasn't in it! she scolded.

Mallon wondered if he would come down that weekend and rehearsed how she would be cool, but friendly, the next time she saw him. He must not kiss her again—she would be lost. Not that he'd shown any desperate need to kiss her when he had left on Wednesday.

She got out of bed on Saturday, determined that she wasn't going to strain her ears that day listening for the purr of his car as she had yesterday.

By ten o'clock, when she realised her ears were at full pitch without her even being aware of it, Mallon took herself off for a walk. But by eleven she was hurrying back—Harris might have arrived while she was out!

He had not arrived, indeed he never did, and she went to bed that night after giving herself another severe talking to.

Mallon woke up on Sunday, showered, dressed and went downstairs to start her day, pushing one Harris Quillian Esquire firmly out of her thoughts. She had better things to do, she decided, than to mope around thinking solely about a male of the species who couldn't even be bothered to pick up the phone to tell her he wouldn't be coming down this weekend.

When the unfairness of that thought hit her—good heavens, she was nothing more than the hired help; why on earth would Harris ring to apprise her of his weekend plans?— Mallon locked up the house and took herself off for yet another walk in disgust.

She determined, positively, that today there would be no rushing back. She had done that yesterday and had been so disappointed for her trouble. Today she ignored the road, deciding to walk over fields instead.

It was two hours later when, not in the slightest hurry, Mallon made her way back to

Harcourt House. It had been good to be out-side. She had picked an armful of wild flowers and grasses and thought how they would brighten up the hearth in the drawing room.

She ambled up the drive and unlocked the front door, feeling certain that she hadn't once thought of Harris—in all of ten minutes. Intending to go down the long hall and into the kitchen, where she would find a vase to arrange the flowers, Mallon was barely through the front door when she heard voices coming from beyond the open drawing room door—one male, one female.

She halted. Her immediate reaction was to break out in smiles—Harris was home. Her next reaction was for her smile to dip. If Harris had brought his sister with him and intended to stay overnight, there was *no way*—he could use whatever excuse he liked, but absolutely, positively, set-in-stone definitely, no way—Mallon Braithwaite was going to share a room with him!

Feeling shy suddenly though striving for an air of pleasant detachment, Mallon, with the intention of popping her head round the draw-ing room door to say Hello, had started to go along the hall when Harris stepped out from the drawing room.

She blushed and caught his glance on her scarlet face. 'Mallon,' he said softly.

'I didn't expect you today,' she blurted out.

'Is it inconvenient?' he enquired, a teasing kind of look in his eyes.

'Not at all!' she answered briskly. Though more gently, 'Is Faye with you?'

He shook his head, and at his next words Mallon's world collapsed. 'I've brought Vivian. Come and meet her.'

Vivian! How Mallon kept her shock from showing, she never knew. It went without saying that he had women-friends. It just hadn't occurred to her that he would bring any of them down here! She smiled and went with him to the drawing room. She did not want to meet Vivian. No way did she want to meet the woman.

As Mallon knew she would be, Harris's lady-friend was an elegant, immaculately turned-out woman. She was a brunette of around thirty—and a sophisticated orchid type. So much for standing there with an armful of wild flowers!

Harris performed the introductions smoothly and with charm, adding pleasantly, 'Mallon has made this place much more like home with her feminine touch.' Mallon, glancing around the sparsely furnished room with its floorboards bare apart from a scattering of rugs, wanted to hit him.

'I'd better put these flowers in water,' she said with a smile—Vivian Holmes hadn't a hair out of place; Mallon had been climbing stiles and scrabbling around picking flowers and grasses. She wanted out of there with all speed! 'Would you like coffee?' From somewhere, the manners borne of her upbringing came to trip her up.

'Love some,' Harris replied. 'I'll just show Vivian around the rest of the house.' Mallon couldn't get to the kitchen fast enough.

Mechanically she got out a large vase and filled it with water, while cruel jealousy threw spiteful darts at her. How could he have brought that woman here? He was showing her over the house, for goodness' sake! How could he?

Mallon's sense of fairness tried to get through. Harris had every right to bring whomever he pleased. It was his property. It was nothing to do with her.

Maybe not, but he could whistle for his lunch if he thought she was going to make it! She was caretaker, not cook. If he was so enamoured of Vivian Holmes that he had brought her down so he could show off his house, then let Vivian cook his lunch—and his dinner too, come to that.

Mallon let go a juddering kind of sigh. Vivian Holmes would probably turn out to be an excellent cook. She looked the type who did *everything* well. Mallon blanked her thoughts off, or thought she had, and then the most horrendous notion hit her. If they were staying here to lunch and dinner—what was to stop them staying the night?

Oh, she wasn't having that! It was for certain Harris wouldn't be expecting her to move out of her room to make way for his 'guest'. Mallon knew, without having to think about it, that Harcourt House, with its two habitable bedrooms and two beds, was just not big enough for the three of them. If Vivian Holmes was staying, Mallon Braithwaite was going.

She had the coffee percolating when she heard them walking about on the bare boards overhead. What were they doing up there? They'd been gone for an age!

Eventually Harris and his companion came down the stairs, and he brought her into the kitchen. Mallon poured three cups of coffee and, while they sat at the table drinking it, Harris invited Vivian's comments on the kitchen. 'Most of the ideas in here are Faye's,' he told her, and somehow Mallon managed to keep her expression even. Vivian had obviously met Faye. Did that signify that Vivian had been Harris's lady-love for some while? Mallon rather thought it did. More than that, Vivian was probably the one with whom Harris spent his weekends when he didn't come down to Harcourt House. True, Faye was under the impression that one Mallon Braithwaite was his mistress, so she might only have met Vivian briefly and have had no idea how serious things were between them. But…

'…and what do you think, Mallon?' Mallon looked across at Vivian and realised that the woman was asking her opinion of the kitchen.

'I think Faye has done an excellent job,' she replied, and discovered, as Vivian pointed out one or two fixtures which could be altered, that, even though the woman was acting as if she was ready to move in and take over at any given moment, her ideas were sound.

More, as Vivian included her in her discussion with Harris, Mallon found that in other circumstances she could quite like her. But that still didn't mean that she was hanging around if Vivian was staying the night.

Though, partly because she was starting to like the woman, and partly from manners, but mainly because she needed to know how long they intended to be there, Mallon queried, 'Will you be here for lunch?' and found herself staring into a pair of gently contemplating warm grey eyes.

But even as her heart did a tiny flip he looked quickly away, his glance resting on Vivian, and for an insane instant Mallon had the impression that he had forgotten Vivian Holmes was there. But, just to prove how insane that thought was, he smiled at Vivian and replied for the both of them. 'I think not. In fact I think we'll get off now. You've seen enough, Vivian?' he enquired, and that, Mallon thought, said it all. Abundantly plain for all to see was that at some later date, when all the work was completed, Vivian was going to move in with him and make Harcourt House her home.

Somehow or other Mallon got through the next five minutes. She was glad they were going. She couldn't be more pleased they were going. So pleased they were going that she smiled as she said goodbye to Vivian, and positively beamed when she said goodbye to Harris-get-out-of-bed-now-Quillian. He hadn't been thinking of Mallon Braithwaite when he had urged her to '*Please,* Mallon. Go now' but an *honourable* man, he'd been thinking of Vivian Holmes, his lady-love!

'I'll see you when I see you,' Mallon called cheerfully, as she watched him follow Vivian out of the kitchen. Honourable! Stuff his honourableness!

She was hurting, but even so she couldn't resist a last look at Harris as he and Vivian went by the kitchen window to his car. Then Mallon promptly turned her back on the window. If he happened to glance through, which of course he wouldn't, then he would see that already he and his companion had gone from her mind and that she had her attention on the kitchen cupboards, in which she was looking for something.

Mallon might not have been looking through the window but her ears were tuned in, listening for the purr of the car's engine, listening to hear it start up and as it departed fade away. Only then would she feel able to let down her guard.

But, listen though she did, and impatient though she was for that sound—for them to be gone—she did not hear any sound of a car's engine. What she did hear was the sound of footsteps—and she froze. They were coming back in!

Fearing that she didn't have another smile left in her, Mallon turned to face the kitchen door. Correction. *They* were not coming back in. Vivian must still be in the car because, tall and straight, and oh, so dear, Harris came in alone.

He came in, came close, and only a couple of feet away he stopped. Silently, and for several seconds, they just stood and stared at each other. Harris fixed his gaze on her and Mallon, sure it wasn't just her imagination, felt a kind of tension in the air between them. She struggled to break it, to find her voice, but her throat was suddenly so dry that her voice came out sounding all husky and sort of choky.

'You—forgot something?'

Grey eyes looked down into deeply blue eyes. 'You—seemed a bit—out of sorts,' he said quietly—and Mallon knew that if this clear thinking man wasn't to guess precisely why she was 'out of sorts', then she had better buck her ideas up.

She did manage to find another smile. 'Who, me?' she queried. Though, because she feared he might be too astute to be fobbed off, she went on, 'How would you feel if you came in looking as though you'd been playing in the dirt and had to shake hands with someone who was the last word in elegance?'

His answering smile was slow in coming but eventually made it. 'It bothered you? Vivian...'

But Mallon didn't want to hear what he had to say about Vivian, and laughed lightly as she told him, 'It's a woman thing.' And again found he was studying her.

'That's all? You're not worrying over anything?' he pressed.

'Not a thing.'

'You're sleeping well?' he queried and, after a thoughtful moment, 'You're not losing any sleep—having bad dreams because I lost my head a little last...'

'Of course not!' she cut in. She did not need him to go into that time they had shared his bed together, thank you very much. 'Good grief, I'm not such a hothouse flower...' She broke off, hothouse flower bringing to mind orchids, bringing to mind Vivian. 'Shouldn't you be going wherever it is you're going?' And please don't tell me where that is because I don't want to know.

Nor did she need it when he suddenly came a step closer and took her hand in his. It wasn't fair because she was melting under his touch— and yet was so weakly in need of his touch that she just didn't have the strength to do as she knew she should and pull her hand out of his hold.

'You're sure you're all right about—everything?'

Oh, absolutely. You in here holding my hand, your elegant girlfriend sitting out there waiting for you—what could be more right? 'Positive,' Mallon answered and, pride belatedly arriving, she pulled her hand out of his grip and took a step away.

'You would tell me?'

Mallon found a light laugh. 'I can see, Harris, that you'd like to set yourself up as my trauma physician. But I just didn't have a problem coming to terms with the fact that, in a given set of circumstances, certain biological urges—er—need to be restrained.'

Any hint of a smile left his expression and Mallon could see that he didn't care very much for what she had just said. But, even so, he stayed long enough to ask, 'May I take it that you've forgiven me my lack of restraint in that department?'

Mallon smiled, a genuine smile this time. If there was a tinge of relief in her smile that she had been thinking *not* about his lack of restraint in the 'biological urges' department but about her own, only she would know about it.

'It's no big issue, Harris, honestly,' she said, and impulsively, quite forgetful that he had his woman-friend sitting in his car waiting for him, Mallon went forward, stretched up, and kissed him.

It was a mistake. She knew it as soon as their mouths touched. A shock of electricity bolted through her. But, as she immediately went to pull back, firm hands came to grip her arms, and she was once more staring straight into a pair of warm grey eyes.

'Th-there!' Mallon whispered on a gasp of breath. 'Completely forgiven.'

Harris continued to grip her arms, then, a second or two later, he said gruffly, 'I'd better go,' and went.

In the following twenty-four hours Mallon went over Harris's visit again and again. Her memories were bitter-sweet. How dared he bring another woman into what was her home? she fumed, in what she knew was an irrational moment. But why shouldn't she be irrational if she wanted to? Why should she be rational? She loved the swine.

But he didn't know that she loved him—nor would he, for heaven's sake! She had seen his sensitivity—she'd just die if he ended up feeling sorry for her. Oh, she wouldn't have that.

Her pride dipped as she recalled the way he had left Vivian in the car and had come back. Mallon sighed hopelessly as she thought of how his fine sensitivity had picked up—for all her efforts to the contrary—that she might be out of sorts about something. He needn't have come back.

Did that mean that he cared? Just a little? Oh, come on, Mallon, for goodness' sake! Did it look as though he cared? Have you forgotten Vivian Holmes? Vivian of the 'I'll show Vivian the rest of the house'. Vivian of the subtle suggestions for alterations to the kitchen. Vivian of the 'You've seen enough, Vivian?'.

Well, if she hadn't, Mallon had. More than enough. Especially when she thought of Vivian moving in and taking up residence at Harcourt House. Mallon went hot and cold all over when it struck her that, for all she knew, Vivian might be planning to arrive, complete with suitcases, this coming weekend!

Mallon awoke on Tuesday morning and knew, without having to think about it any more, that this was the end. She glanced at the wall that separated her room from Harris's room and knew she just wouldn't be able to bear it if Harris and Vivian came down on Saturday and stayed overnight—in his room.

Mallon left her bed knowing indelibly that, before Vivian moved in with her suitcases, she, Mallon Braithwaite, would be moving out with hers.

Before Bob Miller had arrived, Mallon had her bedlinen and towels in the washing machine and had been on the phone to the railway station checking train times. There was a train departing at twelve-fourteen which would deposit her at the railway station in her mother's home town.

It was early to ring her mother, but not too early to pack. Mallon tried to be positive as she got her belongings together and fought to keep unwanted thoughts at bay. But the knowledge that she was severing all ties with Harris and would never see him again was crucifying, so that when at eight-thirty she dialled her mother's telephone number Mallon had never felt so unhappy.

'Hello darling,' her mother answered her greeting, and sounded so warm and wonderful that Mallon almost burst into tears.

'Can I come home?' she asked chokily.

'Are you crying?' Evelyn Frost asked in alarm.

Crying, weeping, bleeding on the inside—yes, all of that. 'Can I come?'

'Of course you can; you know that,' her mother answered and, when she had never been the practical one, she put aside any concern she felt and surprised Mallon by asking, 'How are you getting here? Do you want John and I to come for you?'

'No, no, that's all right,' Mallon replied, and, feeling more in control now, 'I'm catching the twelve-fourteen train—and I'm not crying.'

She went in search of Kevin after her call. 'No problem,' he answered when she had said that she needed to be in town for midday and that if he were going that way any time would suit.

With the assurance that Kevin would give her 'a call', Mallon took her suitcases into the kitchen. She made sure everywhere was as tidy as it could be, given the circumstances, and with her laundry tumble-dried, ironed and put away by ten-thirty, she went to look for Bob Miller.

She found him just as he was about to drive off to another job he was working on some miles away. She explained, cheerfully and with a smile, that she was leaving Harcourt House and had thought, even though she knew he had some keys, that she would leave her set of keys with him.

His expression said he was curious, but when Mallon wasn't any more forthcoming he pretended to be aghast as he quipped, 'You mean you're going—leaving me to make my own morning tea?'

'You'll survive,' she replied, and, after arranging to give the keys to Kevin for him to pass on to him, she returned to the house.

She was undecided what to do about letting Harris know he had lost his caretaker. She wanted to phone him; she had his number. But he might not be in, or in a meeting and unavailable. He had been so good to her, taking her in the way he had and giving her shelter. The least she could do in return was to try to speak personally to him. Though what reason for leaving she was going to give she had no idea. It positively wouldn't be the truth, that was for certain.

In the end Mallon took out her writing paper, knowing that the only reason she wanted to ring him was because she was looking for an excuse. She was aching for the sound of his voice. And that really *was* pathetic! She must be strong, and strong started here.

There was not much time to spare when, with difficulty, she at last managed to write her note. She thanked Harris for his kindness, but stated that she felt now was the time to move on. She sealed the envelope knowing she wouldn't be seeing him again so he would not be able to question her decision. To think that he would do was, she realised, just so much pie in the sky—then Kevin came into the kitchen.

'Do you want these putting in the van?' he asked, seeing her cases down by the door.

'I'll carry one,' she answered—and just then the telephone rang.

'I can carry these, no trouble,' Kevin assured her. 'I'll see you when you've finished on the phone, no sweat.'

He had disappeared before Mallon could decide whether or not she wanted to answer the phone. But who did she think it would be, for goodness' sake? She had been churned up inside about leaving before the phone had started to ring; she was doubly so when she went to answer it.

Her mother had insisted that she and John would pick her up from the station when she arrived. But her mother hadn't consulted John about it. Perhaps they'd discovered John had to be elsewhere at that time. Perhaps her mother was ringing to say for her to take a taxi from the station after all.

She was certain that it would be her mother—so why was she feeling so shaky? 'Hello?' she enquired down the mouthpiece.

'How's life in sunny Upper Macey?' Harris asked, and Mallon had to sit down.

He sounded so warm, sounded in such good humour. 'Fine,' she answered. 'Actually…' She couldn't get the words out.

'Actually?' he queried and, as astute as ever, his tone changing, 'What's happened?' he wanted to know.

'N-nothing. The roof's still on.'

'What's happening—with you?' he insisted, and she knew she was imagining it, but he made it sound as if the house could fall down for all he cared—so long as she was safe.

Oh, wishful thinking! She knew then that she was going to have to tell him. 'I'm leaving,' she announced bluntly.

'Leav…' He broke off, and, obviously looking for reasons himself, 'Has Phillips been around again?' he demanded. 'I know he's working from home this week. If…'

'He hasn't been near,' she replied quickly, guessing that knowledge had reached him from Faye.

'Then what…?'

'I—just think it's time to go, that's all,' she butted in, and, loving him, wanted him to beg her to stay.

'You're not afraid? Nothing's upset you? I haven't upset you? If…'

'It's not you,' she said quickly. Oh, how could she lie to him—how could she not? 'And… And I'm not upset.'

'You are!' he contradicted forcefully.

'I just think…I want to go.'

There was a short silence. Then, 'We'll talk about this at the weekend,' Harris decreed. 'I intended to come down on Friday…' Alone?

'I'm leaving—now,' Mallon cut him off— and very near had her ears blasted for her trouble.

'*You can't!*' he roared.

So she was a good caretaker! Tears pricked her eyes as she quietly replaced the receiver. The phone rang again. This time Mallon did what she should have done the first time. She ignored it. She went to the kitchen and tore up the note she had written. It was no longer needed.

Having locked up as far as was practicable, bearing in mind that the builders would want to come in and out, Mallon went out to the van with the phone still ringing in her ears. Kevin kept up a lively chatter all the way to the railway station, and once there insisted on carrying her cases on to the platform.

'Are you coming back?' he asked as Mallon handed him her set of keys.

'I may do,' she answered, and thanked him and said goodbye, knowing that she had just uttered the biggest lie of all. She wouldn't be going back. She had left Harcourt House for good. It was a permanent leaving. And—it hurt.

Proving that the second telephone call must have been from Harris, her mother and John were at the station to meet her and Mallon had no need to take a taxi.

Her mother looked worried, but Mallon could not bear that anything should blight her mother's new-found happiness so hugged her, and kissed John, and told them cheerfully, 'It's good to be back—but I'm not stopping too long.'

'You know you're welcome for as long as you like,' John replied. 'It's your home now.' Mallon smiled at him for saying so, but knew she would make her own home somewhere else.

Once they were inside the house John carried one of her cases up to the room her mother had prepared for her and Mallon took the other case. 'I'll leave you to settle in,' John said with a contented smile, but while he went back down the stairs her mother stayed behind.

'What happened, Mallon?' she asked. Perhaps because she was so happy herself, she had observed that, for all her daughter's cheerful front, underneath Mallon wasn't at all.

Mallon straightened from the suitcase she had just unfastened and looked over to the dear soul who, since her marriage to John, seemed to have grown in confidence and no longer needed her daughter to protect her. 'I...' Mallon began, ready to evade the question. But, looking at her mother, found it impossible to lie to her. 'I fell in love with him,' she said simply.

'Harris Quillian?' Mallon nodded. 'And he?' her mother asked.

'He has a lady-friend. I thought it best to leave,' Mallon replied.

'Oh, darling,' her mother cried, and came and gave her a hug.

Mallon dully carried on with the business of living. Later that day she was helping prepare the evening meal when her mother slipped up and mentioned that they had been going to eat a little earlier because...

'Because?' Mallon queried, smiling at her parent's look of guilt but eventually dragging from her that her mother and John had tickets for the theatre that evening, but had decided against using them.

'We don't think it will be much of a play after all,' Evelyn Frost ended.

'That's why you booked your seats, was it?' Mallon teased, and, fully aware that the only reason they had decided not to go was because she had come home, she said firmly, 'I wouldn't hear of you not going.'

'But—you're upset!'

'No, I'm not. I was,' Mallon agreed—her mother had known that much. 'But I'm all right now.'

It wasn't easy to persuade her mother that she would be more upset if they stayed home than if they went to the theatre, but at last her mother gave in and they had an early meal.

The house was quiet after her mother and new stepfather had gone and Mallon knew she should be glad of the peace and quiet. But, although the builders would have left Harcourt House for the day now, she had grown used to having them crashing and banging about the place, and wanted to be back there. Though a second later and she owned that, in all honesty, it wasn't the builders' racket she wanted to get back to—just the house.

Harcourt House where, at any given moment, Harris might telephone. Where, at any given moment, Harris might drive up, might arrive, walk in. She half wished she had not left, but knew that alternative: to have stayed and heard, endured, watched his relationship with Vivian Holmes would have been untenable.

She had been right to leave. Mallon stiffened her backbone to endorse that firmly, but that didn't make it hurt any less. She had cut Harris out of her life, left him—without any forwarding address. He might guess she had gone to her mother's new home, but he had not the remotest idea where her mother lived, and neither did he know her mother's new name. Mallon bit her lip hard as fate cackled— Harris was likely to come looking?

She was glad she had insisted that her mother leave her to see to the dinner dishes. Aside from not wanting to give her parent extra work, it gave Mallon something to do. She felt she needed to keep busy; it might help her to stop thinking of Harris Quillian.

It did not. By eight-thirty the kitchen was immaculate. Mallon went to the drawing room and over to one of the comfortable chairs, but no sooner had she sat down than she stood up again. She couldn't settle.

She went upstairs for her book and came down and read one paragraph—and found her thoughts had drifted off to how Harris hadn't wanted her to go. Her insides went all soft on her when she thought of how he'd said, 'We'll talk about it at the weekend. I intended to come down on Friday'. Malevolent intelligence reminded her that he might well be intending to visit Harcourt House—but not alone.

Which was precisely the reason why she had left—because she knew she wouldn't be able to bear seeing him with Vivian Holmes. It wasn't mere jealousy, Mallon knew that, torturous though jealousy was. It was more—self-preservation. If he was going to be happy with Vivian, good luck to him. She just didn't want to be around to witness it.

Feeling despair starting to descend on her like some dark cloud, Mallon once more pushed Harris out of her head. Positive. Be positive, she willed herself, and determined that she would set about making herself a new life. First thing tomorrow she would check with the agencies, buy a paper and see what situations were vacant. She…

The doorbell sounded. Her mother hadn't said she was expecting anybody to call. Mallon left the drawing room and went along the hall. With her fingers on the door lock, her thoughts on telling whoever it was that she'd be pleased to take a message for either her mother or John, Mallon pulled back the heavy front door—and got the shock of her life!

She went scarlet, then, as her colour began to fade, she went pale. The caller was there for neither her mother nor her stepfather. But tall, business-suited, and with grey eyes that weren't looking in the least friendly, there stood the man she had only recently mused had no earthly idea where she had gone!

'H-how—did you find me?' Mallon gasped. Her colour might be returning, but her brain seemed incapable of thinking further than that.

Harris Quillian stared uncompromisingly down at her, 'With difficulty,' he gritted. 'And not a little abandoned pride.' And, his glance searching her face, though what he was looking for she hadn't a clue, 'I need to talk to you, alone,' he stated in clipped tones. 'We'll talk in my car,' he informed her tautly.

CHAPTER EIGHT

MALLON was still staring at him, totally stunned, when Harris took a step back, as if expecting her to step forward to go with him to his car. 'You w-want to talk to me?' she questioned faintly—about as much as she was able to manage as her brain started to function again and one thought after another chased through her head: how had he found her? He hadn't known her mother's new address—or even her old one for that matter. Why had he bothered? And—what was there to talk about?

'I do,' Harris answered grimly, repeating succinctly, 'Alone.'

Alone? Without her mother and her husband there? Did that mean that Harris wanted to give her a ticking off for leaving without notice? Surely not? Though it sounded very much that way. From the tough look of him he wanted to give her a 'telling off', but intended sparing her the humiliation of taking it with others present.

'I...' She opened her mouth to tell him what he could do with his 'telling off', but—and she admitted she was weak where he was con-cerned—she didn't want him to go away again—not just yet. Soon enough he would walk away from her life for ever. 'You'd—um—better come in,' she invited.

'I said, alone,' Harris reminded her shortly.

'My mother and John are out. Unless you intend to murder me, we can talk alone inside.'

The answer she received was a kind of grunt. But when she half turned, Harris took a step forward. She held the door while he crossed the threshold and, closing the door, she led the way into the drawing room, her heart still hammering away at seeing him so totally unexpectedly.

Once in the drawing room she turned to face him, intending to challenge why had he both-ered to come to see her. But as her glance went to his face, grim still and without a doubt hos-tile, he was, even so, very dear to her.

'Have you eaten?' she found she was asking instead. From his business suit she guessed he had come straight from his office.

'Who wants food?' He spurned her offer none too politely. So it was to be pistols at dawn? She could have asked him to take a seat, but it didn't look as if he would be there that long. 'Why did you go?' Harris demanded abruptly.

He wanted an explanation—she didn't have one; her brain was seizing up again. 'I was never going to stay!' she responded. Then, gaining her second wind, 'You knew that,' she challenged. 'You knew that the job was never going to be permanent.'

Harris looked back at her, annoyed with her, she knew. Then, suddenly, as he looked into her deeply blue eyes, his harsh look seemed to soften and he ventured, 'I thought we could talk—you and I?'

Oh, Harris, don't! She needed to be tough, and he was making that difficult. 'We—could,' seemed to be forced from her. And remembering, 'I've discussed things with you, told things to you that I've never told another living soul. But...' Feebly, she broke off. Broke off, feeling that she had said too much, that already she had said *much* too much.

'So what happened to that?' he wanted to know. 'What happened to that trust you had in me that you had to run away without even talking to me about it first?' His glance was fixed steadily on her when he accused toughly, 'You wouldn't have let me know anything about your plans had I not chanced to telephone!'

Mallon didn't like his digging, his chipping, nor that 'run away' statement. 'Will you have a seat?' she said in a rush. 'Perhaps I can get you a drink if you don't want anything to eat.'

She did not like it, either, that he saw too much when he instructed harshly, 'Don't be nervous with me, Mallon. I don't like it. Especially since you know I would never harm you.'

If only that were true! She was harmed. She did hurt; he was the cause. She went over to one of the well-padded chairs. Although it seemed he had refused her offer of a drink, when she sat down Harris, closer than she would have liked, came and took possession of a chair next to her.

There were only a few yards separating them when, still searching to exonerate herself without giving herself away, Mallon thought she could safely explain, 'I did write you a note.'

'I didn't find it.'

'You've...?' He'd been down to Harcourt House? 'I—er—after your phone call... When

I told you I was leaving—well, there didn't seem any point in leaving a note. I tore it up,' she said. But found that the question she had previously denied would not stay down. 'You've been to Harcourt House?'

'Of course I've been there!' he grated—and proceeded to totally astonish her when he added shortly, 'I was halfway down there when Bob Miller contacted me on my car phone to say that you'd already left. It seemed to…'

'Just a minute!' she interrupted on a gasp of sound. And when she could see she had his full attention, she went on. 'Bob Miller wasn't there when I left!'

'I know he wasn't.'

Mallon wasn't sure her jaw did not fall open as something else all at once struck her. 'You didn't—didn't—um—leave your office to go down to Upper Macey just because…?' She broke off. Of course he hadn't! Love must have softened her brain. 'I'm sorry, that was a stupid question.' Grief, he dealt in million-pound deals—as if he'd desert his business just because she'd told him she was leaving!

But, 'I did,' she clearly heard Harris reply. And, if that wasn't enough to have the blood pounding in her ears, he caused emotional colour to flood her face when he added, 'I delayed only long enough to contact Bob Miller on his mobile, then I took off.'

'Y-you t...?' Words failed her. She supposed she had been a competent caretaker, even a good caretaker, but *that* good? So good that Harris would leave his business to charge down to Upper Macey to see her, to ask her to reconsider? No—common sense reared its sharp hand to give her a slap—don't be ridiculous. She was a caretaker, not some high-flying executive at Warren and Taber Finance. 'You—said you rang Bob Miller.' She managed to latch on to something fairly sensible.

'I rang his mobile. He wasn't at Harcourt House but at one of his other jobs some ten or so miles away.' Mallon had known that. 'He said you had discussed handing over the keys into his safe-keeping.' Harris paused and then, with that steady grey-eyed look she knew so well, said, 'I didn't care at all for the finality of that.' Her lovely blue eyes widened slightly. 'I told him to get back to Harcourt House immediately and to stop you from leaving.'

Fresh shock made her gasp. 'Stop me from leaving?' she echoed faintly.

'By the time he got there, you'd gone.'

Mallon's insides were having a wild time within her, her emotions haywire as she strove to be calm and to tell herself that Harris was a kind and sensitive employer and that he would act so towards any member of his staff. But, against that, her brain was insisting, Oh, come on, Mallon, do you really believe that? But if she didn't believe that...then didn't it follow that for Harris, a businessman of some note, to drop everything to chase down to see her, to try to stop her from leaving, it must mean—mustn't it—that he cared a little for her?

Her mouth did fall open in shock. Even as she was discounting that Harris could possibly care, the notion caused her some shock. 'You—er...' was as far as she could get before her brainpower returned to scoff. As if! 'You—er—decided to carry on down to Harcourt House anyway?' was the best she could come up with—that much had already been established when Harris had referred to not finding any note from her when he'd got there.

'It was my only option,' he answered, his eyes steady on hers. 'When I realised I didn't know where in blazes you were heading, that I had no address, apart from somewhere in Warwickshire—and then only if you were making for your mother's new home—I was left hoping you might have left some clue to your whereabouts in your room or somewhere else in the house.'

'You checked my room?' she questioned faintly, trying desperately not to see anything in Harris's actions that just wasn't there.

'I checked everywhere,' he replied.

'Nothing?'

'Not a clue!' he answered heavily.

Oh, heavens, it sounded as if he had been quite keen to find her! 'B-but, you did find me.' She smiled, still trying to show a cool front. 'You're here now.' And because, even though her insides were all of a tremble, her curiosity would not stay down, 'How *did* you find me?' she just had to ask.

Harris seemed to relax just a trifle for the first time since he had arrived, and with a hint of a smile answered, 'As I mentioned, with difficulty, and not a little abandoned pride. Though I have to say that a little abandoned pride was well worth the cost if it meant I could find out what I wanted to know.'

Crazily, her heart just refused to listen to the logic of her sober brain, which cautioned, This can't mean what you think it means—that Harris cares a little for you. 'My address?' she queried, her voice barely above a whisper.

'Your address,' Harris confirmed. 'I was in the drawing room, those wild flowers you picked on Sunday still fresh in the hearth, as I tried not to despair that I might never find you.'

Had he not referred to his visit on Sunday in the same breath as his despair that he might never find her, Mallon thought her heart would have leapt straight out of her body. But he had mentioned the two together and, by reminding her of Sunday, when he had brought his woman-friend, Vivian Holmes with him, it negated for Mallon any crass thoughts and feelings she might otherwise have had.

'I—er—must have left some clue after all,' she commented stiffly, and saw Harris frown at the change in her.

But, determinedly, he kept to his purpose, although by then Mallon was confused as to know what purpose that was—she certainly wasn't going back to be his caretaker again. Then he revealed, 'I was quite desperately trying to think of anything you had ever said that would hold a clue. I knew your old home was in Warwickshire, and that was about it. So I went back to the very beginning, how we'd met when you ran away from my brother-in-law. But still couldn't find any clue. That was until I remembered how you'd said you had written to Phillips applying for the job. The moment that I realised Phillips had once had your old address, I was on my way to see him.'

'Oh, Harris!' Mallon murmured involuntarily, realising then that this was what he'd meant by abandoning a little pride. It would have gone very much against the grain for him to ask Roland Phillips for anything. 'You—must have wanted my address pretty badly.'

Harris looked at her for long, long seconds, his expression unsmiling. 'I did,' he said simply.

Her throat went dry. 'He—er—gave it to you without any—er—fuss?'

Harris did smile then. 'I wouldn't say without any fuss. Though to begin with he said that if you'd written he didn't know where the letter was. When I told him you'd done some filing in his study…'

'You remembered I'd told you I cleared up his study?'

'Didn't I say I went over everything you'd ever said, looking for clues as to where you might be?' He did not wait for an answer, but continued, 'After a short discussion that went along the lines of Phillips still having a job when his employers heard from my company if he didn't let me loose amongst his files, he allowed me into his study.'

'You found my letter in a file marked General Correspondence?'

Harris nodded. 'Then I had to sit outside your old address for a couple of hours, waiting for the new tenants to come home in the hope they had your mother's forwarding address. But, after that, the rest was relatively easy.'

Mallon stared at him, a roaring starting in her ears. Surely she could no longer deny what everything was telling her—that Harris did care—a little?

'You—went to all that trouble?' she questioned huskily.

Harris looked levelly at her. Then, quietly, he told her, 'It was important to me.' Mallon's eyes were fixed on nowhere but him when slowly, carefully, he added, 'You are important to me, Mallon.'

Such a rush of emotion hit her then that she couldn't sit still, and she jerked to her feet. Keeping her back to him, so he should not read the flood of emotion in her face, she took some steps away.

She was vaguely aware of hearing him move. Then knew he was close behind her when, over her shoulder, he soothed, 'Now don't be alarmed. I know I came on too strong when we shared a bed a week ago, and if that's what frightened you away we'll take things more...'

Mallon turned to face him. He looked worried, strained, and it was too much. If she was the one to be left with her pride in ashes, so be it. Even though she still found it difficult to believe that he'd dashed down to Harcourt House, sunk his pride to go and ask his detested brother-in-law for a favour and had then come to look for her—how could she let Harris think himself the villain of the piece?

'Oh, Harris,' she said softly. 'What a poor memory you have of that morning.'

He stared at her, but that look of strain did not lessen. 'I didn't terrify the life out of you?' he asked.

She shook her head, and even managed to find a smile. 'So, okay, I'll admit I'm not the smartest in the—er—bed department, and that I've probably got a lot to learn there. But, as I remember it, you were the one who ordered me out, not the other way around.'

Some of the strain seemed to go from him, but he was still questioning when he asked, 'And nothing that happened that morning has worried you, made you feel awkward, ill at ease with me…?'

'The only thing that has been bothering me is that, while I knew that I could doubly trust you, I discovered that I…' She hesitated. However, he seemed to be suffering too, and she loved him too much for that. 'I discovered that I couldn't—er…' She took a breath, and plunged. 'I couldn't trust myself.'

Harris stared at her for perhaps one age-long second, Then he said softly, 'My dear, are you saying that, had I not turned you out, you'd have willingly…?'

'I couldn't have stopped myself,' she admitted honestly.

'Oh, love,' he murmured, and stretched out his arms for her. Her heart fluttered wildly as she went to him. She felt his arms about her and it was sheer bliss to be held by him. 'Is that why you ran away?' he leaned back to ask, looking deeply into her eyes. 'Because you didn't trust yourself alone under the same roof with me?'

He did care! He must care, mustn't he? Everything about him, every look, everything she knew about him, said that he wouldn't be here now, holding her this way, if he didn't care. But, while Mallon knew that she trusted him completely, a modicum of self-preservation lingered, and she found that she could not be as open with him as he perhaps would have liked.

'Not—quite,' she admitted after some moments of staying silent.

'You ran away for some other reason?' Harris queried, as sharp as she knew him to be. Mallon felt then that she would prefer not to say anything else at all. To do so would be to tell him that she loved him and, while she was growing more and more to believe that he did care a little for her, that was a long, long way from the totally deep and all-consuming love she had for him. 'You're not going to tell me, are you?' he asked gently. 'Not even when we've always been able to talk, you and I.'

She laughed lightly and had no idea when her arms had gone around his waist—it felt so good, so natural just to be standing there holding each other like this. 'There are some things a girl doesn't even tell her best friend.' She smiled.

He smiled too, and then bent to gently kiss the corner of her mouth. 'Not even,' he said on straightening, his grey eyes warm on her, 'when you know that—I've fallen for you—in quite a big way?'

Involuntarily her eyes shot wide. Her throat went dry as she looked back at him. Oh, Harris, Harris, Harris, I love you so. She checked. Steady. This was all so incredible. Steady. What did 'fallen for her in a big way' mean, exactly?

'You—um—wouldn't care to expand on that a little, I suppose?' she asked, having to search and find every scrap of control.

But he looked equally wary, before manfully biting the bullet. 'If I know my Mallon, you wouldn't issue an invitation like that un-

less you have some kind of—feeling for me.'
Oh, my word, he was getting close.

She hesitated. 'S-so?' she stammered, realising, even as she said that small word, that it
was tantamount to admitting that she did have
some kind of feeling for him.

He knew it too, she realised, when his grip
on her tightened before he allowed himself a
small smile. Then he said, 'It began one rain-
soaked day when I stopped to offer you a lift.
You refused at first…'

'But you did a circuit and came round
again,' she supplied in a whisper.

'I told myself I was being stupid—some-
body else would have come by and you'd have
accepted a lift with them. But was that rain on
your face—or tears? I was in no particular
hurry.'

'You took me in,' she said softly. 'Not only
gave me a lift, but gave me a job too.'

'Why wouldn't I?' he asked, and, his expression going grim, he continued, 'Phillips,
regrettably, is linked to my family—and you'd
been assaulted by him!'

'You were so kind.' Mallon smiled, and, because she didn't want him looking so grim, she

leaned forward and stretched up and gently kissed him.

'Oh, Mallon, Mallon,' Harris murmured when she pulled back. But his grim expression had gone and there was a trace of a smile on his face when he went on, 'I don't know about being kind. All I thought I was doing at the start was doing my small bit to get you back on a more even keel after your distressing experience. What I hadn't anticipated I'd be doing would be spending so much time in the week that followed with you so much in my head.'

Mallon stared at him in delight. 'You thought of me sometimes?'

'Often,' he replied. 'That first Saturday when I came down to Harcourt House it somehow didn't seem to sit well with me that I was there and you were in a hotel.' He smiled as he confessed, 'I know I couldn't settle until I'd come to get you the next day. For my sins only to be annoyed that, while I'd been thinking how you must have been put off men, you'd been spending time with some man named Wilson!'

'Wilson?' Mallon queried. 'Oh, Tony Wilson!' she remembered.

'How could you?'

'How could I what?'

'Here am I, growing all irritated over the man—and you can barely remember who he is!'

'You're—irritated over…?'

'I believe it's called jealousy,' Harris replied, a light of such tenderness in his eyes that her heart seemed to turn right over.

'You were jealous?' she asked incredulously. 'But we barely knew each other.'

'My dear,' Harris replied softly, 'there just isn't any logic to the way I feel about you. I was glad one minute that there wasn't a phone in the house so Wilson couldn't call you. But I couldn't get a phone installed quickly enough to stop Phillips coming around with telephone messages. I was, by turns, jealous, then angry. But I knew that I liked to find you at Harcourt House so much that I didn't care at all for the notion of you packing with the intention of spending a second weekend at the Clifton Hotel.'

'You asked me to stay,' she recalled.

'And,' he took up, 'when I couldn't resist giving in to my need to kiss your irresistible mouth, I had to pretend that the need was yours.'

'You rat!'

'Love me?'

Mallon backed away from that one. 'You were saying?'

Harris took time out to gently touch his mouth to hers. Then, his grip on her firming, he drew back to say ruefully, 'I shouldn't have done that. Just as I shouldn't have kissed you that Saturday when we both had the idea of taking a shower.'

'I remember.' She smiled. Would she ever forget it? It was the night she had realised she was in love with him.

'That was the night I told you that you were in no danger—but didn't think to mention that—I was.'

'You were in danger?'

'Of falling in love with you, my darling,' Harris murmured tenderly.

'Oh,' Mallon whispered on a gasp of breath.

'I wasn't admitting it—not then,' he owned.

'Of course not.' Had he really said he had been in danger of falling in love with her?

'But I had never felt like that before—as if I was losing some of my control. I realised I needed to leave in order to sort myself out.'

'And did you? Sort yourself out?'

'Not then. All I knew then was that the moment I was apart from you I wanted to be back with you. I was constantly pulled to go down to Upper Macey—and was constantly fighting it. Only when I recognised what my true feelings for you were did I see that, while visions of your beautiful body threatened my self-control, it wasn't just your body I was enamoured with but you and your inner loveliness.'

'You're—enamoured of me?' Mallon asked shyly.

Harris looked down into her face, seemed to love looking at her, and then said tenderly, 'Dear Mallon Braithwaite. My darling Mallon Braithwaite. What do you think it is that I've been telling you for the last ten minutes if it's not that I love and adore you to total and complete distraction?'

'Oh, Harris,' she sighed.

'Do you mind?'

'Not at all,' she answered breathlessly.

'And—do you think you could love me a little in return?' he asked carefully, going urgently on when she seemed too shy to answer, 'I know you've been harmed in the past, but I'll never harm you. You know...' But Mallon, while feeling more than a little euphoric, was suddenly bombarded by a recollection of how she had felt bruised and harmed by his visit a couple of days ago. All warmth for him left her face. 'What's wrong?' Harris demanded at once. 'Tell me...'

'What's your relationship with Vivian Holmes?' Mallon butted in, her rosy feeling of belief in his love starting to painfully crumble.

'I don't have a relationship with her!' Harris denied, without having to think about it.

'That's why you brought her down to Harcourt House last Sunday, was it, because you don't have a relationship with her? That's why you showed her all over the house, asked her if she'd seen enough, listened to her...?'

'Vivian Holmes is one very well thought of interior designer,' Harris butted in this time.

Mallon's mouth formed an 'O'. 'But...' she began, though as she started to relive the time last Sunday Vivian being an interior designer did seem to fit. 'You didn't say,' Mallon ar-

gued as she got herself together a littl[e]
would have thought you'd have mentione[d]

'You're right, of course,' he agreed, an[d]
corners of his mouth started to curve in a
of a self-deprecating smile. 'And norma[lly]
probably would have said she was an in[terior]
designer come to have a look around.
you'd got me in a stew, Mallon,' he confe[ssed]

'I—had?'

'Believe it, my love. I'd so wanted to
you, yet knew I should stay away. But I [had]
to come to see you because I couldn't sta[y]
away. For the first time in my life I felt vulnerable. There have been times when I just
wanted to quietly hold you, and others when
I've quite desperately wanted to make love
with you. It was after our lovemaking a week
ago that I started to feel I could no longer trust
myself to be alone with you and began to grow
fearful that you might leave if the same thing
happened again. Yet what guarantee did I have
that, in that obstacle course of a house, some
other floorboard might not trip us up or some
other minor accident would occur, and, alone
with you there, I might find you in my arms?'

Mallon stared at him thunderstruck. 'You—
brought Vivian Holmes down because...'

Because I couldn't stay away any longer. ...ugh it was Faye I rang first to ask to come ...me because I felt I shouldn't risk being ... with you.' He smiled then. 'I was in a ... about you—but you'd been through ...gh, my darling.'

...allon had a feeling that if Harris went on ...this for much longer her backbone was ...g to melt. 'But—Faye didn't want to ...e?'

...She'd got some business she was in the ...iddle of, and since I'd merely asked if she fancied just coming along for the ride, not making anything big of it, of course...'

'Of course.' Mallon found she was smiling again. 'So you rang Vivian...' She broke off when Harris shook his head.

'I was growing more and more desperate to see you, and in the process of wondering if I dared risk going down to Upper Macey anyway, Faye rang to say her friend Vivian had just phoned for a chat during which—Faye in the past apparently having gone into raptures about Harcourt House—Vivian said she was just dying to see it.'

'That's when you rang Vivian?'

Harris placed a tender kiss to the side of Mallon's face. 'That's when I rang her. I told her I had my own ideas about the place but that I'd welcome hearing any suggestions she had to offer. So...' his look became rueful '...I came and I saw you, and I felt some gigantic thump in my chest when you came in looking absolutely adorable with your arms full of wild flowers, and I wished Vivian Holmes a hundred miles away.' He smiled then as he added, 'I wanted you all to myself, Mallon Braithwaite.'

'You came back,' Mallon said softly. 'You left Vivian in the car and came back.'

'I needed some time alone with you. And you kissed me, and I wanted to hold you, and to go on holding you. I, my dear, was feeling more vulnerable than ever.'

'You—w-were?' Mallon asked shakily.

'Oh, yes,' he owned, and confessed, 'Which left me having to return to London when I didn't want to go at all. Which consequently had me making plans to go down to Upper Macey at the weekend and deciding—if you weren't happy with me sleeping under the same roof—to pick you up from the Clifton early in the morning on Saturday and Sunday. Only…'

'Only?' Mallon prompted, her head spinning, her heart racing with all he was saying.

He kissed her again, and held her that little bit closer. 'Only I couldn't wait until Friday evening to hear the sound of your voice.'

'Ah,' she whispered. 'So—you rang me at Harcourt House this morning.'

'And knew—the instant you said you were leaving—that I couldn't let you. That I love you with everything that's in me. That I can't let you go.' Harris paused to place a gentle, almost reverent kiss on her brow before going on, 'When I realised that I didn't have a clue where to find you I broke out into a cold sweat. I had to find you. Life without you, my dear love, would be unbearable.'

'Oh, Harris!' Mallon sighed.

'Does that mean that you're—glad I found you?' he wanted to know.

Mallon laughed lightly; she just had to. 'You know I am,' she answered.

'As in—you love me a little?'

Oh, she loved him, loved him, loved him. 'As in—I love you a lot.'

'Oh, my darling,' Harris breathed, and, as if he had been holding himself in check for far too long, he drew her close up against his heart and held her so for long ageless moments. 'You're sure?' he asked urgently, pulling back to look into her face.

'I've been sure ever since that night we shared the same shower room,' she answered honestly.

'You knew *then*?' He seemed astounded.

'There were indications along the way,' she replied. 'But that was when I knew.'

'Sweet love,' he breathed, and kissed her, held and kissed her, and kissed her again, until at last he drew away and, with his arms around her, guided her over to the sofa where they sat close. Then he kissed her again, and said those magical words she thrilled to hear. 'Mallon, Mallon, I love you so,' he told her, and when she bathed in the glow of his love but was too choked to say anything, he prompted, 'And you…?'

Mallon beamed—and found her voice. 'And I love you, so much,' she answered, and kissed him, and was kissed in return.

'Thank heaven!' he murmured, and, after holding her close for many minutes, confided,

'I didn't know whether I should call here to-night or early in the morning. But my soul was in torment, and it just seemed beyond me to leave seeing you until tomorrow—even if,' he added with a lopsided kind of grin, 'I was unsure of my reception.' She smiled lovingly at him, and he went on, 'I stood there, when you opened the door, desperately trying to gauge from your expression if I was about to make the biggest fool of myself of all time.'

'Oh, Harris!' She had never thought to hear him sound so uncertain over anything. 'Thank you for braving it,' she said from her heart, and admitted, 'I've been in a bit of—er—torment myself, over you.'

'Oh,' he breathed softly. 'I'm so very sorry.' As though to wipe away any pain she had endured, he tenderly kissed her. But, looking into her eyes, his expression grew solemn. 'Why did you try to leave me?' he asked. 'You are going to tell me?' he pressed.

Mallon went a little pink as she confessed, as she knew she must, 'I thought that if you came down to Harcourt House at the weekend you might bring Vivian Holmes with you. I'm sorry, Harris, but the thought of you and her s-sleeping in the room next to me was more than I could take.'

Harris was hugging her close up to his heart before she had finished. 'Oh, sweetheart,' he murmured. But, drawing back to look into her sunny blue eyes, 'You were—jealous?'

'You sound surprised.'

He grinned cheerfully. 'Such a notion had never occurred to me.'

She kissed him because she loved him. She could hardly believe what was happening, and because she wanted to see his face she drew back this time. Then she heard the sound of a car on the drive.

'It sounds as if my mother and John have come home early. Um…'

'Um?' Harris queried.

'I—er… Well, my mother wanted to know what had happened to bring me home. I told her I was in love with you…' Harris's beam of a sudden smile caused her to break off. But she felt she had to tell him the rest before her mother came in. 'I also told her that you had a lady-friend.'

'You meant Vivian Holmes?' Mallon nodded, and he smiled and said, 'Then, my darling, it looks as if I shall have to untell her. Perhaps I'd better do that before I ask her.'

'Ask her?' Mallon queried when he didn't add anything.

'Well, I suppose it's your mother I ask. Though it could be your stepfather. Do you know?'

'What?' Mallon asked, by then feeling totally confused.

'It's customary, I think, to ask a parent for the hand of their daughter. I've never done this before, but I'd like to get it right.'

'Hand?' Mallon queried faintly.

'We are getting married, aren't we?' he asked, his expression all at once never more serious. Mallon swallowed hard, her heart thundering. She hadn't thought... 'You will marry me?' Harris pressed. 'I won't rush you if...'

'I'd love to marry you,' she answered chokily.

He exhaled a held in breath. 'Good. Thank you, my love,' he murmured, and, bringing her left hand to his mouth, he kissed it. 'Perhaps by the time we come home from our long honeymoon Harcourt House will be ready for its mistress.'

Mallon gasped. 'Me?' she said in wonder.

'Only you,' Harris replied, and tenderly kissed her.

'Oh, Harris,' Mallon cried. Mistress of Harcourt House, wife to its master! Oh, how wonderful!

MILLS & BOON® PUBLISH EIGHT LARGE PRINT TITLES A MONTH. THESE ARE THE EIGHT TITLES FOR AUGUST 2002

———— ❦ ————

THE SHEIKH'S CHOSEN WIFE
Michelle Reid

THE BLACKMAIL BABY
Penny Jordan

THE PREGNANT MISTRESS
Sandra Marton

TO MARRY McKENZIE
Carole Mortimer

THE BRIDE PRICE
Day Leclaire

HIS PRETEND MISTRESS
Jessica Steele

A CONVENIENT WEDDING
Lucy Gordon

THE NANNY'S SECRET
Grace Green

MILLS & BOON®